LIMF

The Choice

The Choice

JOANNA ERLE

ROBERT HALE · LONDON

ISBN 0 7090 7758 0

Robert Hale Limited
Clerkenwell House
Clerkenwell Green
London EC1R 0HT

2 4 6 8 10 9 7 5 3 1

Typeset in 11/16pt Souvenir
by Derek Doyle & Associates, Liverpool.
Printed in Great Britain by
St Edmundsbury Press, Bury St Edmunds, Suffolk.
Bound by Woolnough Bookbinding Ltd.

For
Lisa, Ian and Glen
Who make all things possible – or very nearly

'Hast though found me, O mine enemy?'

1 Kings

CHAPTER ONE

As her fingers closed about the handle of the door into her draw-ing-room, Louise Treharne hesitated. For a moment she shut her eyes. Took a deep breath. Then she entered.

On the far side of the modishly elegant room a man's tall figure stood silhouetted against one of the three long sun-bright windows. He was looking out into the quiet London street, but, as the door closed, he turned. The April brightness behind him left his face in shadow.

In a doubting whisper Louise said, 'Harry?' and then again, more hopefully, 'Harry, is it really you?'

'Yes. Harry.' Stark words, harsh tone. He made no move towards her.

She, however, closed the distance between them in a rush and flung her arms about his neck. 'Harry! Oh, Harry! After all these years!'

A moment or two passed before he responded and his arms went round her. 'What's this? Forgiveness?'

She looked up at him, her eyes wet with tears. 'No! Oh, no! I never believed what they said. Never!'

'Then you must be the only one. Father believed it.'

'He did not want to. But he said everything pointed to you.

9

Then when you disappeared— He thought it confirmed your guilt. He felt your loss though, Harry. Truly he did! More and more as the years went by and there was no word from you.'

'But still thought me guilty.' He made a small sound of disgust. 'I was never a liar. He should have remembered it. As for my disappearing— There were others anxious to put a noose round my neck. I chose not to wait until it was in place and had no intention of giving anyone a clue where to find me. You, Louly, were scarce out of the schoolroom.'

'Louly! Only you called me that. Oh, how I missed you! Wept for you! My kind big brother. Never for a moment did I think you guilty. How could I? You were my hero. I tried to persuade Papa . . .'

Taking one of his hands in hers, she turned to pull him towards a sofa. 'But it's past. All over. You're safe and you're here. Come and sit down and tell me who found you and how they knew where to look when no one else did.'

He stopped abruptly, gripped her hand more tightly and swung her round to face him. 'No one found me. And what do you mean, *it's all over*?'

'But isn't that why you've come back? Because you *know*?'

He pulled his hand free from hers and stepped aside. 'It seems I don't.' The harshness in his voice was more marked. 'I'm here for one reason only: to settle accounts with Anthony Daunton.'

Louise stared up at the dark uncompromising face she could see plainly now. 'But how can you?' she said breathlessly. 'He's dead.'

'*Dead!*' Bitter protest and anger rang together in the word.

'Oh, do come and sit down. I'll have Garrard bring you a drink. Madeira? Brandy? Anything you like. Have you eaten?' She was already at the bell-rope.

'Brandy. No food.' He moved a chair close to the sofa, waited

10

until she was sitting down before seating himself. Rubbing the crease between his eyes, not looking at her, he said, 'Wait until we're not likely to be interrupted, Louise, before you tell me what it is I don't know.'

The pretty clock on the mantelshelf ticked loudly into the silences between the butler's double journey. Harry tossed down the brandy the man had poured and poured another before he said, 'Well, let me have it. Start with Daunton. When did he die? How? He would be only forty-four now.'

Watching him with troubled uncertainty, Louise told him, 'It was about a month ago. A shooting accident. Though there was a lot of doubt in view of his mountainous debts and the depositions he left regarding you. But there was no clear evidence he had taken his own life and he was given the benefit of the doubt.'

She paused and he said roughly, 'Go on.'

'He cleared your name, Harry. Gave chapter and verse of the fact that you had left both the room and the club before that horrid young man was murdered. He confessed he knew that there was someone else in the room with Lorimer and that he kept quiet about it because it was his own young brother. He said that the shock of learning her younger son was a murderer would have killed his mother who was already ill.'

'So he protected his family at the expense of mine! I suppose I must be glad our own mother was already dead since he was prepared to let me hang in his brother's place.'

'Oh, no, do not say so! He could not have intended that!'

His laugh jarred her. 'You think that having gone so far, when it came to crisis point he would have stepped forward to save me? At cost to his mother and brother?' He sprang to his feet and strode away to the window again.'

After a lengthy silence, he turned to say, 'A fine family the Dauntons! Where is the brother now? Lionel, isn't it?'

11

'He died two years ago in the same cholera epidemic that killed Father.'

Slowly, he came back to stand with his hands gripping the back of his chair. 'So . . . Daunton, his brother, my father, all dead and out of reach. And the thought that kept me going through the bitter early years, Louly, was of the day I would come back to beat the truth out of Anthony Daunton and throw the evidence in my father's face! Lorimer's murder was no surprise to me, but it was not in my nature to have raised a hand against such a contemptible wastrel. Or anyone else. But that was then! If I could reach Anthony Daunton now, *him* I think I could kill!'

'He did set the record straight in the end,' Louise offered, in sad mitigation.

'You think I should be grateful to him? I was twenty-two when he tossed me to the wolves! As full of plans for the future as any man at that age. His vindication comes twelve years too late. *And it's not enough!*' he finished savagely.

Several minutes passed in silence after that, but suddenly he moved round the chair, sat down and said more calmly, 'I should not be troubling you with my ill feelings. Tell me, how did you fare after I left, Louly? Father was expecting Treharne to declare himself at the time. It appears he did. I knew how deep in love you were and feared he would hedge off because of the scandal, but there was nothing I could do about it. If I had stayed to be hanged, everything would have been ten times worse for you. Was it very bad?'

'For a time. Some people— Well, you know how it is. But Robert spoke for me in that same awful week. Papa asked him if he had fully considered the matter and Robert told him that what had happened could not affect his feeling for me. He said, too, that with what he knew of you he did not for a moment think you had murdered Lorimer. So you see, I wasn't the only one.'

12

'I must improve my acquaintance with your Robert.' But the expression on the lean, brown face yielded nothing to the words and his next question held a cynical undernote. 'Are you as happy with him as you expected to be?'

She nodded. 'Above my deserving.' Putting her head on one side, she regarded him pensively. 'You've changed, Harry.'

His mouth twisted. 'Twelve years is a long time and, as I said, the first five before I found my feet were hard. Harder than I can tell you. Unprepared as I was, the lessons of survival were learned painfully. But I did learn . . . I was lucky . . . and in time, I prospered.'

'What will you do now? You're Lord Verrell, head of the family, you realize. Well, you were not surprised when I mentioned Father's death, so you must do. How did you discover it?'

'An English newspaper someone passed on to me. It was already two months old when it reached him. He had no way of knowing there was anything in it of personal interest to me. He knew me only as Adam Lang.'

'The name on the card you gave Garrard . . . I did wonder.'

'I scribbled *Harry* on it to give you a clue.'

'I thought it might be just news of you. But I would have welcomed even that. Did you not think of coming home when you learned Papa was dead?'

'With a noose still waiting for me as far as I knew? No. As for the title. . . ' He shrugged.

'Father did not change his will, you know. You inherit all that he always intended you to have.'

The lines of Harry's face tightened still more. 'Dammit, Louly! I don't want his money or his property! Don't need it. I wanted his belief in me. His trust. Those I *did* need!'

'It was hard for him. Everything was against you.'

'*You* believed me innocent, so you say. My father knew me . . .

13

or should have done. Should have known what I would and would not do.'

'He wanted to believe you: I know he did.' She saw the sceptical flick of his brows and rushed on, 'It's past, Harry. For your own sake, let it go. Tell me what you mean to do now? Go home to Surrey? To Mardens Hall?'

'To Surrey? I've no idea. I've been Adam Lang for a long time, and in the better years, a merchant of Chittagong, of Calcutta and elsewhere, trading in emeralds, jade and silk. It will take time to step back into being Harrington Verrell again. As for Mardens Hall . . . no, not there. The memories are too bitter.'

'You are welcome to stay here with Robert and me as long as you care to.'

'That's good of you, Louly. Thank you. But no, there are things I must do – think about. Your news has thrown me out of my stride. Some of my commercial interests will have to be wound up. First though, I need to see Dickman if he is still the Verrell man of business?'

She nodded. 'If you have to return to India and those other places, you will come back to England after, won't you?'

'If Dickman confirms my innocence is officially recognized, yes.'

Louise smoothed the silk of her skirt, glanced at her brother's grim face, said appeasingly, 'Sir Anthony left a daughter, you know. I believe she is only seventeen. She has had to face all the scandal of the uncertainty surrounding his death, his confession of concealing evidence and an overwhelming burden of debts. Everything is in the way of being sold. Her home, its contents, everything! The poor girl is penniless and would be out in the street if a country vicar, or someone of that sort, had not offered her shelter. So Aunt Sophy writes, though how she knows, I cannot think.'

'Well, don't expect sympathy for the chit from me. Coming from the family she does, I don't doubt she'll survive and prosper. Most likely at someone else's expense. God above! I thought her father was my *friend!*'

'He was ten years older than you,' Louise said at a tangent.

'If you are saying I was young enough and foolish enough to be flattered by his interest, I probably was.'

The biting self-contempt in his voice brought Louise's gaze up to his face again. So like and so unlike his remembered image. There was a cold, measuring watchfulness in the grey eyes that the younger Harry's eyes had never had; nor could she remember the bones under the sun-dark skin having hinted at so harsh a face in maturity. He looked as though he rarely smiled, she thought, or if he did, the humour would be mocking, unkind. More sadly than before, she said, 'You *have* changed, Harry. More even than I first thought.'

His eyes, so like her own in shape and colour, so unlike in their expression, narrowed and glinted. 'I had change thrust on me, my dear. But I'm a good deal wiser for it.'

His tone offered Louise no reassurance. She said hesitantly, 'I may not be putting this into quite the right words, Harry, but I think you need to take care.'

He considered the remark, frowned, and dismissed it with a shrug.

CHAPTER TWO

The clang of Herriards' iron gates as the bailiff's man closed them behind her, seemed to Lucy Daunton to have a dreadful finality. It was as though they sounded a last discordant note in the passing-bell for her old life. The distressing circumstances of her father's death, his confession of having suppressed evidence that would have cleared a man of the charge of murder and all the rumours and scandalmongering that followed had numbed her. She had endured the troubles that had descended on her as a result in a state of dazed disbelief. But they had been all too real; as real as the uneven cobbles of Chalworth's main street she could feel through the soles of her shoes. All that remained of her old life was on the carrier's handcart behind which she was walking as it trundled towards the rectory and she seemed to sense that with each step she took the person she had been crumbled away a little more.

Who was she now that she was no longer Miss Daunton of Herriards, daughter of Sir Anthony Daunton? Those two things had defined her, given her standing. Now, without family, home, money or distinction of any kind, what would happen to her? What would she become?

She glanced at the calm-faced woman walking beside her and

16

met an encouraging look. 'The worst is over, Lucy, my dear. Today is the beginning of a new life and you know we at the rectory will do our best to make it a happy one.'

But she did not want a new life, she wanted to be safely back in her old one: back in her dearly loved Herriards of which she had been queen; wanted her pretty pony, Pearl, the familiar servants and all the small freedoms and pleasures that had gone to make up her days. She blinked back tears and said with the careful politeness instilled in her by her governess, 'Yes, I know. Thank you, Cousin Rothwell.'

Mrs Rothwell was a very distant cousin of her father's, she knew, so she had every reason to be grateful to her and her husband, the rector, for offering her a home. But it was strange to her to be in an inferior position and she was not sure how well she would conduct herself in the new role.

'As I have said to you before, Lucy, Susan will be happy to have you again for a friend . . . almost a sister, so close as you are in age,' Mrs Rothwell chatted on.

Susan! Not for a moment did Lucy believe Susan would be happy to have her either as a friend or a sister. There had been friendship between them when they were children, but Susan had grown up into a stiffly wary girl with a censorious eye, ever ready to take offence. Lucy stifled a sigh.

'Well, here we are.'

Jimmy, the carrier's younger son, had already turned the handcart into the semi-circular gravelled sweep before the rectory and brought it to a stop by the porch. A maid came out to help with the boxes and Mrs Rothwell led Lucy into the comfortable country house.

Susan was waiting in the broad hallway. Eighteen months older than Lucy, more than two inches taller, honey-brown hair, clear green eyes and regular features, she was generally allowed to be a handsome girl. But Susan was as much aware as anyone that beside Lucy, her looks faded into insignificance. There was no competing with eyes so large and darkly brown, lashes so long, such a neat little nose and beautifully shaped mouth all set in a delicately oval face under shining black curls. It was far from pleasing to know that from now on her appearance would always be judged in comparison.

Without approaching near enough for Lucy to expect an embrace, Susan said in a dutiful tone, 'Welcome, Cousin Lucy. I hope you will be happy with us.'

'Thank you, Susan,' returned Lucy as dutifully.

The girls' lacklustre meeting did not escape Mrs Rothwell's notice, and she sighed with regret for their lost friendship. With a quick glance of warning at her daughter, she said, 'Take Lucy upstairs, Susan, and show her where things are. Jessie will bring up the boxes very soon.'

Treading the stairs in Susan's wake, Lucy swallowed hard against the pressure of tears. She had expected Susan to resent her coming and she did. How terrible it was to be an object of charity. Even a father rarely at home was better than none at all. Her father . . . No, she must not think of him now or she would dissolve in misery.

Following Susan into one of the upstairs rooms, Lucy looked round. Though in no way cramped, it was half the size of the room she was used to occupying. The furniture was simple but attractive, the curtains made of a pretty chintz and a flower-bordered carpet covered most of the floor. With surprise however, she saw there were two half-tester beds.

'Does someone else sleep in here?' she asked.

'I do. It's *my* room!' Susan's tone was sharp-edged.

'Oh. I've never shared a room before,' Lucy said unthinkingly.

Susan fixed her with a gleaming, hostile look. 'Nor have I.'

Lucy flushed. Guarding her tongue was clearly something she must learn to do.

Crossing the room to open a cupboard door as Jessie, the youngest of the rectory's three house servants, entered with two of Lucy's boxes, Susan said pointedly, 'We shall be sharing this closet, too. I've emptied three shelves and made space for you to hang your gowns.

'Thank you. Will Jessie unpack when she returns with the rest?'

Susan curled a contemptuous lip. 'No. That is something you will have to do for yourself. Jessie has quite enough work to occupy her.'

Her frown deepened when Jessie returned with two more boxes. 'You seem to have brought a great deal with you! I can't imagine where it is all to go. You will need to put it away very neatly or neither of us will ever be able to find what we want – and that's something else *I'm* not used to.' On that sour note, she marched out of the room.

Taking off her black swathed bonnet, Lucy sank on to the bed Susan had indicated was hers. The calamity that had overtaken her a month ago had been overwhelming. Would she ever forget the day when her white-faced governess had told her that her father had been found shot in the small woodland on the eastern boundary of Herriards' parkland? An accident, Miss Tressick had said; he had tripped and fallen while out shooting for the last of the pheasant before the breeding season began. But when the size of his debts was discovered and the news-sheets learned of the affidavits regarding his withholding of evidence twelve years ago, there had been ugly rumours. She could thank the rector for being among the first to give her father the benefit of the doubt and for having so speedily arranged his interment in the family tomb, which, as a confirmed suicide, he could not have been. But then, as soon as the funeral was over, the bailiffs had moved into Herriards and her world had fallen into final ruin.

It had taken Susan's sharp little jabs of unkindness to bring home to her how far-reaching was the change that had over-taken her. Though her father had come to Herriards only occasionally, preferring to live in London among his gambling friends, when he had come down, he had been the kindest, most indulgent father in the world. She had been lapped about with luxury, surrounded by servants, who, having an easy life, had been willing enough to humour her wishes. Lucy had never understood why her earlier friendship with Susan had cooled, but when they reached their teens, Susan had seemed to change, to withdraw her goodwill. Lucy had then turned to other girls for companionship, in particular to Jane Bellmore and Charlotte Molyneux, both of whom lived in the neighbouring village of Ashwick.

Even so, she had not been prepared for quite such an open show of animosity from Susan. It looked as though things might be worse than she had expected.

Swallowing the threatening tears, she began to unpack, plac-ing everything with great care.

Mrs Rothwell was in the dining-room setting the table for the light midday meal usual at the rectory, a task assigned by custom to Susan.

'You're soon down,' she said, as her daughter walked in.

Susan turned to take napkins from a drawer. 'I thought it better to leave Lucy to settle in,' she said.

With a slight frown, Mrs Rothwell took in the stiffness of the back so carefully turned to her. 'I hope you are being kind to her, Susan, as I asked you to be.'

Setting out the napkins, Susan kept her face averted. 'It's not

easy, Mama. She gives herself such airs! So shocked to be sharing a bedchamber! And Jessie, of course, was to do her
unpacking.'

'That shouldn't surprise you. You know very well she is accustomed to servants doing everything for her.'

'Yes. And I remember Papa saying none of them had been
paid a penny this past year!'

'That is not Lucy's fault. Think what a distressing time it has
been for her. Sir Anthony was far from being a satisfactory father,
but he was the only close relative she had. Lucy has suffered
shock after shock. Her father's death, the manner of it, the suspicion of suicide. . . Then to find that he had led a life of such
reckless extravagance that her home and everything in it is to be
sold. Now, instead of the gaiety of a London season and the
come-out she was to have this year, she finds herself penniless,
dependent on the charity of others for a home.'

Seeing no softening in her daughter's face, Mrs Rothwell's
voice took on a sterner note. 'I've said very much the same thing
to you before, Susan, and I expect you to keep it in mind. Lucy
is only seventeen. She—'

'She's not. She was eighteen three days ago,' Susan interrupted.

'Oh, poor girl! I had quite forgotten her birthday is in April.
Even so, she is young for her age, having been shut away from
the world so much. And being of small stature people tend to
think she is younger than she is and treat her accordingly.'

'Oh, yes! Everyone babies and pets her!'

'That is much less likely to happen now. Nor will she find it
easy to adjust to losing the consequence of being Miss Daunton
of Herriards. Remember, my dear, you are a year and a half older
than she is. Unlike Lucy, you have had the good fortune always
to have a loving family around you. Your expectations, too, are

now superior to hers. That alone should make you more generous towards her.'

Susan spun round, her colour high. 'She wasn't very generous
to *me* when she *was* Miss Daunton of Herriards. *I* was not the
one asked to go with her to the balloon ascent which I so longed
to see! No, on occasions like those she always chose Lady
Vauncey's granddaughter, Jane Bellmore, or Charlotte Molyneux
who is niece to the Earl of Quinstock! *I*, being only the rector's
daughter, was asked to join her when she had nothing exceptional to do and needed company.'

Mrs Rothwell frowned. 'But not necessarily for the reason you
suggest. It was chiefly Miss Tressick who had the choosing of
Lucy's companions. With Sir Anthony living almost entirely in
London after Lady Daunton's death, Lucy was in her governess's
charge. Miss Tressick was a clever, well-intentioned woman, but
her ideas tended to be rather grand . . . snobbish even. And that's
something else for which Lucy cannot be blamed.' She sighed.
'You seemed to like each other well enough when you were children. Perhaps you will come to do so again.'

Susan shrugged and hid her angry eyes.

The little clock on the mantelshelf struck twelve, drawing Mrs
Rothwell's attention away for a moment, then with crisp finality
she said to her daughter, 'Lucy needs all our kindness, so please
try for a more generous spirit towards her, Susan. Now go and
see how she has managed and tell her it is time to come to table.'

A month later the rector gently broke the news to Lucy that
Herriards was sold with all its remaining contents. No one knew
who had bought it because the business had been done through
a firm of lawyers. Herriards' gardeners had been retained to keep
up the appearance of the place, and a week after news of the sale
became public property, a middle-aged man and his wife arrived

to act as caretakers. The Penfolds were unknown to anyone in the village and kept very much to themselves. If they knew the name of their employer they did not reveal it.

With the news, it seemed to Lucy that her last link with her old life had gone and each succeeding month as it passed brought her new lessons in restraint and forbearance. She tried to show the world a brave face, but at times her spirits plummeted. She could not help contrasting the pleasures of the balls and routs and picnics that would have marked her entry into London society and to which she had been looking forward so much, with her present days punctuated by making her own bed, searching for eggs when Mrs Rothwell's hens laid abroad, sewing flannel petticoats and baby clothes for the poor, or being asked to take a basket on her arm like a servant and walk to the village shop to make purchases for the household.

She was, of course, still in mourning for her father, but would she, she wondered, ever have use for the one or two pretty gowns already made for her in preparation for her move to London? And what was to happen to all those carefully polished accomplishments proper to a young lady . . . the joyfully learned dances . . . her repertoire of songs . . . the conversational French? But harder to accept than any of this was the abrupt ending of her piano lessons. Her teacher, Professor Lowson, had considered her skill to be exceptional and she had both studied and played with passionate delight. Now she could not even practise. Susan had made her very much aware that the rectory piano was *hers*, little though she used it. Pride would not allow Lucy to touch the instrument unless particularly invited to do so by the rector or his wife for their evening entertainment, and then she played only the shortest and simplest pieces that showed no noticeable difference from anything played by Susan.

Susan remained a hard cross to bear. Their relationship had

settled into uneasy civility. But it was a civility growing ever more stretched by nursed grievances as spring passed into summer.

Early in September, on a day of golden sunshine, Mrs Rothwell called the two girls to her.

'This afternoon I shall be busy with Cook making jams and preserves, but with such an abundance of fruit this year I should like you two girls to carry some to the poorer villagers together with some sugar where needed. You, Susan, know which villagers are most in want. Jessie is putting up the baskets for you now, so go and put on your bonnets. It's a beautiful day for a walk.'

With glum resignation, Lucy followed Susan upstairs to their room.

Doom fell on the expedition as soon as Susan discovered the silk roses on the bonnet she wished to wear crushed by an encroaching hatbox of Lucy's.

'Look at this!' Susan turned furiously on the other girl. 'What right have you to treat other people's property with such selfish disregard! These roses cost money – if you can understand what that means. It's time you thought about it. Your present silks and satins won't last forever and you can't expect *my* papa to replace them!'

But for that final remark, Lucy would have apologized with sincerity. As it was, she said off-handedly, 'I'm sorry. But the roses are not so very creased. The warmth of the sun will probably smooth them out.'

Clamping her lips together, Susan flung the bonnet on her bed and chose another. In simmering silence they went down the stairs, picked up the baskets from the hall table and set out.

Lucy had given little thought to the superiority of her clothes. The Rothwells were comfortably circumstanced rather than rich, but the rector gave generously to charity and Susan possessed just one silk gown for 'best' day wear, one silk ball gown and two

24

pairs of carefully hoarded silk stockings. The humiliating reminder that Lucy was now dependent on the Rothwells' generosity, cut deep.

They walked towards the poorer end of the village in unforgiving silence. The basket on Lucy's arm seemed to grow heavier with every step and the loveliness of the day made her long to hurl it into the nearest hedge and be off over Sugarloaf Hill on her pretty little Andalusian pony. But Pearl had been sold with many other things that she had once thought indisputably hers . . . .

Entering the first of the cottages they were to visit, Lucy was shocked into forgetting her own griefs. Miss Tressick having passed on a terror of catching unspecified 'things', she had never before crossed the threshold of one of the poorer villager's homes. This initial experience appalled her as she took in the smoke-blackened walls, the presence of a bed in the only downstairs room and the grimy poverty of what passed for bedding on it.

Though not all the cottages were in such a beggarly state, the last two they visited could only be described as hovels.

As they left, forgetting to preserve her silence, Lucy exclaimed indignantly, 'How do people survive in such places? Broken windows, holes in the roof, *water* actually rising through the flags in this dry weather! Is no one responsible for repairs?'

Susan made a small, scornful sound in her throat. 'Most of the houses we have seen today are part of the Herriards estate. Perhaps the new owner will do what your father never did.'

'He cannot have known their condition!'

'Oh, indeed, he did! Before last Christmas my father remonstrated with the Herriards' steward over it. The poor man was himself upset at his inability to put repairs in hand. Sir Anthony had told him he had better uses for his money and prohibited any work being done.'

Lucy came to a stop in the middle of the village crossroads. Though her father's visits to his home had been rare, he had come laden with gifts. Looking at the other girl with dislike, she said, 'Then I don't think he was telling the truth. My father was the most generous of men!'

Susan's glittering gaze clashed with hers. 'Yes, but in two directions only. Towards himself and towards you. And costing *him* little or nothing. Did you ever give a thought to the dressmaker who bought the silk for your gowns? Who spent hours, days, making them and was never paid?'

'No, I did not, because I did not *know* people were not paid!' Lucy almost choked on her helpless anger. 'But don't think I don't know *why* you are saying these things. It's because you are eaten up with envy! It's what made you such a wry-faced thing when you came to Herriards. Always looking sourly down your nose. I *hate* living with you!'

It had become a schoolroom squabble fuelled by old resentments. Lucy dropped her empty basket at Susan's feet. 'You may take that with you because I am not going a step further in your company!' Cheeks aflame, she turned and walked rapidly away from the other girl.

CHAPTER THREE

She walked blindly along a lane that led out of the village into the countryside. She had gone some distance before her emotions began to steady and her pace slowed. Only then was she able to admit that it was the likely truth of what Susan had said that had stung most.

From the age of six, when her mother had died, her father had been all she had, or knew, of family. Accustomed from birth to being cared for chiefly by nurse and governess, she had recovered fairly quickly from the loss of her mother. It was later, as her understanding developed, that she missed her deeply. She realized now that it was following her mother's death that the pattern of her father's lengthy absences had been established: remembered, too, how much his occasional and erratic visits had meant to her. A handsome, charming man, for the two or three days he remained when he came to Herriards, he had made her the centre of his attention and those days had been magical.

Sadly it came into her mind now that for all his charm, he had been a deeply selfish man. And his final and most selfish act had been to leave his young daughter to face alone all the horrors of his death, his bankruptcy and the scandal of suppressed evidence in a case of murder.

She still grieved for him, would still miss him, but with a clearer view of his character, the idol was damaged and she realized that it was Herriards that had provided her childhood with its greatest sense of security. She had loved every rose-red brick of the house; loved its dark shining oak floors and tall traceried windows. If she had been lonely there, she had not known it, for wandering through its many rooms she had peopled it with her imagination. And under Miss Tressick's reasonable rule she had been sovereign lady of all. She ached to be back in its safekeeping, to have its familiar trappings around her. But that safety could never be hers again. It was time to stop looking back, to stop drifting through the days. Her relationship to the Rothwells was too tenuous to continue to accept their generosity indefinitely. She must think more positively about what she could do to support herself. Whatever it was, it was unlikely to be either easy or enjoyable, but apart from the financial independence finding a situation could give her, she would escape from Susan.

For a long time she sat on a sunny bank in a secluded corner just thinking and struggling with the difficulties of how to find a way to support herself. The choice was depressingly meagre; there were just two options for a girl of her sort, she could either be a governess or a companion. Neither could be said to have much appeal. But at least she had been well taught and in the past five months she had learned something of patience and resignation; enough, she hoped, to fit her for either post.

The shadows of the hedge trees lengthening across the grassy field before her warned her how far the day had advanced and that she had more immediate problems to face. What was she to say to the Rothwells when she returned – as she must – to the rectory?

Reluctantly, she rose to her feet and turned back towards Chalworth. When she reached the first isolated cottage she realized she was now on a lane that followed the eastern border of Herriards' parkland and gardens. Soon she glimpsed the tall, twisted chimneys among the treetops where they glowed in the last of the sunset. Overwhelmed by a longing to see her home again, she crossed the lane to put her hands on the top of a nearby close-boarded estate gate to pull herself on tiptoe in an effort to see more of the house. She had expected the gate to be bolted as usual, but surprising her, this one gave inward, its weight tugging her a step or two on to the path beyond.

She hesitated only a moment. She was so late a few more minutes could make no difference and, as the new family had not yet come to take up residence, there were only the caretakers in the house. If she kept to the shelter of trees and bushes no one need know she had entered the grounds.

As though drawn by a charm, Lucy walked along the well-known path. There could be no harm in just looking, she told herself, and with the light beginning to fail there was less and less chance of being seen.

Where the lilac trees that bordered the path ended, she halted.

The sun was down now, the sky beginning to flush into rose and lavender and across a stretch of lawn she could see the house, its colour darkening as the dusk gathered. There was no glimmer of light in any of its many windows. Wherever the Penfolds were, they were not in the rooms on this side of the house. Suddenly bold, Lucy crossed the grass and stepped on to the terrace.

The long latticed window she was facing, opened, she knew, from the smaller drawing-room in which stood her desperately missed pianoforte. Though she had been told that a number of items had gone to auction, most of the furnishings had been bought with the house and she wondered if her piano could still be there.

Stepping nearer, she peered in through the ancient, wavy, leaded glass. It was darker still inside and the room hid its secrets under dust covers. She pressed closer . . . .

Roaring out of nowhere, a black monstrous shape hurled itself at the other side of the glass in an explosion of furious sound.

Breathless with shock, Lucy leapt back, spun round and launched into panic-stricken flight.

She did not hear the window opening, had no preparation for a tremendous thump between the shoulder blades that slammed her to the ground and jolted the remaining breath from her body.

When the head of a huge black animal was thrust into her face, sheer terror overwhelmed her and she knew no more.

Sound being the first sense to return after unconsciousness, Lucy was aware of the voices and what was being said some moments before she was fully sensible.

'I can't find she's come to any more harm than being frightened into a faint, sir.' That was a woman's voice close by. 'I'd never have opened the window for Juba if I had known it was a young lady out there, but with the light so far gone it wasn't possible to see what he was so excited about.'

Further off, a man spoke, his tone caustic. 'An unlikely *lady*, Mrs Penfold, creeping around private property and peering in at windows. More likely some tinker's brat sent to spy out a weak point for a break-in. It's a pity Juba didn't inflict a bite where it would make it painful for her to sit down for a week or two to teach her a lesson.'

Light was penetrating Lucy's eyelids now and they began to flutter.

'I think she's coming round,' the woman said.

'In that case I'll be off. I've delayed long enough,' said the stringent male voice. 'Now don't be soft with her, Mrs Penfold.

30

She can have had no good purpose prowling around after sunset, so threaten her with the constable and despatch her with a flea in her ear. I'll send Penfold in to back you up.'

The slam of a door jerked Lucy's eyes open. She was, she realized, in the room into which she had been peering, lying on a sofa from which the dustsheet had been removed. A lamp stood on a nearby sheeted table and a plump, middle-aged little woman in a grey bombazine gown stood staring down at her with a would-be stern expression on her pleasant face.

Licking dry lips, Lucy said in an aggrieved, if rather shaken voice, 'I'm not a tinker's brat.'

'So you heard that, did you! Well, *I* didn't think you were, because I never yet saw one in silk stockings and lace-trimmed petticoats such as were on display when Juba knocked you over. But I got to you before the master and made things seemly, so he didn't see what I saw.'

'The master?' With the woman's help, Lucy struggled into a sitting position. 'But he has not come. I mean everyone says the new owner isn't living here yet.'

'Maybe. Which isn't to say he's never to do so. But that's neither to the point. What *is*, is what *you* was up to, young miss?'

Glancing round the room, more sadly than she knew, Lucy said, 'I used to live here. I was walking nearby and found a side gate open and came in just to look at the house once more. And then I wondered if my piano was among the things bought for the new owner. But I could not see easily and when I pressed against the window some awful thing almost came through the glass at me.'

'So that was the way of it!'

Mrs Penfold's swiftly changing expressions reflected some knowledge of Herriards' former occupants. Giving up all pretence of sternness, she said, 'You must be Miss Daunton then. I'm sorry

Juba gave you such a fright. If the windows weren't leaded, I think he would have gone through the glass. Not knowing who was outside, I opened the window for him'

'Is Juba a dog? He seemed the size of a lion.'

Mrs Penfold nodded. 'Well, he's not small, though the master says he is young and could grow larger. He's gone off with him now, so you don't need to worry about seeing him again. But how does a young lady like you come to be out alone with darkness coming on? I take it you're living in the village still?'

'Yes, at the rectory.' Guilty recollection flooded in on Lucy and she said worriedly, 'I'm much later than I meant to be. I expect they are wondering where I am.'

'So I should think! As soon as you feel able—' She broke off as the door opened and a man a few years older than herself came into the room carrying an ancient fowling piece and trying to look fierce.

'You can put that thing down, Penfold,' his wife called to him more sternly than she had spoken to Lucy. 'This is Miss Daunton who used to live here and only came to look on her old home, so all's well. Just as soon as she's feeling quite the thing, you can walk her to the rectory which is where she lives now.'

Conscious of being at fault, Lucy's dread of her reception mounted with each step of the way back to the rectory. Penfold left her at the gate and she went slowly up the path to the house. All the Rothwells were in the hall when Jessica opened the door in answer to her knock. Being met with relief instead of being overwhelmed with reproaches was worse, in a way, than what she had anticipated and her apologies for having thrown the house into turmoil were heartfelt.

The rector allowed her to make only a brief sketch of her wanderings before suggesting in his quiet but authoritative way that as no one had eaten yet, they sit down to their belated meal at once and keep the servants waiting no longer. An early night would benefit them all, too, after so much excitement, he said, and further discussion of the afternoon's events could wait until the next day.

Susan, surprisingly pink-nosed and red-eyed, had not spoken to Lucy since her return and nothing was said between them as they went upstairs together. However, when the door of the bedroom was closed, she turned to Lucy and said in an odd, stifled voice, 'I thought you'd run away for good.'

'Where would I go?' Lucy asked sadly.

'Yes . . .' Susan bit her lip. 'I'm sorry, Lucy. I should not have said what I did about your father. Or the rest.'

Stiffly spoken though they were, the words sounded sincere and evoked a quick response from Lucy.

'I'm sorry, too. I said more than I meant and truly I did not mean to cause so much trouble.'

'Since Papa said we were not to talk about it until tomorrow we had better say no more. Except' – Susan sighed heavily – 'I'm glad you're back safely.'

Once in bed, it was with relief Lucy blew out her candle and closed her eyes. Yet, tired as she was, sleep did not immediately follow. Thoughts and impressions streamed through her mind, centred on what had happened at Herriards.

Indignation surged through her again as she recalled the harshly scornful voice dismissing her as a *tinker's brat* and following that with the vulgarity of his regret that Juba had not bitten her in an unmentionable place! It would not have been possible for her to *like* whoever it was had taken possession of her beloved home, but to know as she did now that the usurper was someone who could make such a remark made it easy to regard him with contempt.

Mrs Penfold had referred to him only as 'the master', she recalled, and she had not thought to ask the woman his name. But there could be no doubt that he existed and visited Herriards.

CHAPTER FOUR

Matthew Chandos Rothwell, rector of St Cyriac's, Chalworth, was a large man, pleasant of face and easy of manner. In his university days he had been a notable athlete, which had not prevented him proving he also possessed a notable intelligence. Those of his parishioners who thought to take advantage of his ready sympathy and generosity had soon learned he was not easily fooled. Early next morning he summoned Lucy and Susan for separate interviews in his study. Lucy first.

There was both sympathy and a hint of amusement in the rector's hazel eyes as he observed Lucy's apprehensive look. Stemming her renewed apologies, he said with a quiet smile, 'My dear, your absence disquieted us all for an hour or two but in the end it was nothing so dreadful . . . a little forgetfulness regarding time and something of an adventure. What concerns me is the point from which it all started – your quarrel with Susan.'

With flushed cheeks, Lucy told him about the crushed hat, her grudging apology and the disagreeable silence in which she and Susan had set out on their visits.

Her eyes downcast, she ended stumblingly, 'And then, on the way back, somehow it – *everything* – just flared up and we said things . . . quarrelled . . . and I went off for a walk.'

The rector nodded at her. 'Yes. That is very much what Susan told us yesterday. Except that she gave a slightly fuller account. An account not much to her credit, I'm afraid. The past six months could not have been happy ones for you and I am sorry to think Susan has not been as kind as she might. But she has had only eighteen months more than you in which to learn wisdom, so forgive her if you can.'

'Oh, it hasn't been all Susan's fault,' Lucy confessed, conscience-stricken. 'I haven't tried very hard to win her good opinion. Have sometimes said things . . .'

'Well, I find some satisfaction in the fact that neither of you has sought to lay blame on the other. It makes me think that if you both try a little harder you might be surprised into renewing the liking you once had for each other.'

It was too soon for Lucy to share his belief, but feeling that agreement was expected, she said, 'Yes, sir.'

The rector's eyes twinkled understandingly, but all he said was, 'Then I think we may now move on to other things. My wife is of the opinion that because you saw so little of your father it would not be too out of the way for you to go into half-mourning. If you are in agreement, then she sees no reason why she should not take you and Susan to a ball at the Ashwick Assembly Rooms in two weeks' time. Which makes it a suitable moment for me to pass this to you.' He had taken a small crimson velvet case from a drawer as he spoke and now handed it to Lucy.

She recognized the case at once and even before opening it, said softly, 'Mama's amethysts! Papa always said they would be mine one day.' She looked up from the pretty violet-coloured stones with a sparkle of tears in her eyes. 'But how – I mean, I thought they had been sold with everything else of this kind.'

'Those I managed to save for you,' the rector said, not revealing that he had bought them at auction for her.

'Oh. I don't know how to thank you! I cannot tell you what it means to me to have something of hers. And these . . . these were what Mama was wearing when her portrait was painted. The one that use to hang—' Memories flowed in on her and she gulped, unable to complete the sentence.

The rector rose, came round his desk and laid a kindly hand on her shoulder. 'Well, there you are, child. Now they are yours, as your papa intended and, I am sure, as your mama would wish. So if that is all settled, run along now and look towards a happier future. Tell, Susan, please, to come to me.'

Answering Mrs Rothwell's enquiry, when her daughter had returned with the two baskets but without Lucy the previous day, Susan had said only that Lucy had chosen to go for a walk. But as the day advanced from afternoon into evening and Lucy did not come, Mrs Rothwell had enquired into her absence more particularly and Susan was driven to confess to her quarrel with Lucy.

Wasting no time on recriminations, Mrs Rothwell had gone to consult her husband, which resulted in Simon, the gardener's boy, being despatched to scour the village and its surrounds. When he returned without any news, the rector had ordered his cob to be saddled and rode out on a wider field of search but with equal lack of success. His return had preceded Lucy's by no more than twenty minutes.

Entering her father's study, Susan was in a greater state of apprehension than Lucy had been. The rector's opening words however, were not quite what she had expected.

'I have no intention of raking over yesterday's coals, my dear, but I think we need to talk. I am sure I know you better than to believe that mere petulance over crushed roses on a bonnet induced so much ill-feeling between you and Lucy. I suspect a deeper, longer-held grievance. If that is so, it would be better brought into the open and a way found to deal with it.'

For some long moments Susan was silent, her inward struggle obvious. At last, in a strangled voice, she said, 'I think it began with the singing lessons, Papa . . . .'

'*Singing lessons?*' The rector looked his astonishment.

'Yes. Don't you remember Señor Contarini remarking on the quality of my voice after hearing me sing at Mrs Hammond's charity concert? He said that trained, it could be excellent.'

Puzzled, the rector said slowly, 'I have some recollection of it. But surely that was three or four years ago?'

'Yes. But you said at the time, that though you were willing to pay for me to attend Señor Contarini's classes in Tilchester each week, the horse and gig could not be spared so regularly.'

The rector nodded. 'Yes, I remember now. But what can all that possibly have to do with Lucy?'

'At the time Miss Tressick took her to Tilchester every week for piano lessons with Professor Lowson. Because he is crippled, he could not go to her. Lucy could have offered to take me with her in the Herriard carriage because she was always allowed to do things like that if she wanted. But she never did!'

A brief pause for breath and she added bitterly, 'She had so much! But the one thing I wanted – *the one thing, Papa!* – which she could have so easily made possible for me to have, she never offered. And what did she *ever* make of her own opportunities? I never heard her play at Herriards and *here*, when you and Mama have pressed her to perform, she has played nothing but the simplest pieces and no more. I know I do not play very well, but if I could have been taught to sing properly, I would have worked so hard and it would have meant so much to me!'

'My poor child, I had no idea how important it was to you. And

38

if *I* did not, I wonder if Lucy did? Did you ask her to take you to Tilchester with her?'

'Well, not precisely. But I hinted broadly several times.'

'She may not have understood what you wished. She could have been no more than thirteen or fourteen at the time – not an age when much thought is given to others. It is I who am at fault for not recognizing what was truly important to you.'

'Oh, *no*, Papa!'

'Oh, yes, my dear. The blame cannot be laid on Lucy's shoulders. But there is something that puzzles me. I recollect hearing that Professor Lowson never accepts a pupil who does not show exceptional talent. I did not know Lucy had been a pupil of his. It is strange that she never uses the instrument in this house unless pressed. Have you any idea why that is?'

For a moment Susan looked blank, but then, remembering how positively she had informed Lucy the pianoforte was *hers*, she flushed scarlet.

'I see.' The rector looked grave. 'It seems I have failed you in more ways than one, Susan.'

Susan found that almost unbearable. Mutely, with tears in her eyes, she shook her head.

Quietly, her father said, 'You must not think, my dear, that in offering Lucy a home, generosity has been entirely on our side. The benefice of St Cyriac's is exceptionally well endowed . . . endowed by the Daunton family originally and in their power to bestow. Your mother's relationship to Sir Anthony was a remote one, yet, when she told him of our wish to marry and our need, he recognized the connection and when the living fell back into his hands, which was blessedly soon, he did not forget and gave it to me. Through Sir Anthony, we have lived here in comfort and plenty in the pleasantest of surroundings. Our lives might have been very different else. Whatever Sir Anthony's faults may have been, this family has much

for which to be grateful to him. So you see, my dear, apart from
Lucy being a very young and inexperienced girl in need of help, it is
a matter of giving and receiving on both sides.'

Ashwick, lying two miles west of Chalworth, was the greater of
the two villages, its small monthly market serving them both, as
did its Assembly Rooms. Built by subscription, the graceful,
colonnaded building had one large, elegantly decorated ballroom
lit by handsome chandeliers, a smaller room for lesser functions,
a card-room and a supper-room. Its appointments and the
manner in which the regular balls held there were conducted,
made it sufficiently well regarded to attract custom from the
discerning of the town of Tilchester, five miles away.

Even so, it was a less magnificent venue for a first ball than
Lucy might once have expected, but she did not repine in the
least as her gaze took in the pleasant scene. The room was
already more than half full, the orchestra, lodged in a bow-fronted
balcony, was tuning instruments and a generous supply of gilded
chairs stood against the white and gold walls. She bubbled with
excitement and pleasure as she walked with Susan and Mrs
Rothwell to a vacant set of chairs: a first ball was a first ball, even
if she had had to submit to her delightful pink gauze overdress
being dyed grey. The resultant dove colour was not as frightful as
she had feared, and though she mourned the pink silk rosettes
that had been replaced by knots of lavender ribbon, they had the
virtue of looking well with the amethysts.

Susan's gown, though lacking the cut and finish of Lucy's, was
a becoming charmeuse embroidered in sea-green about the neck
and hem, a colour that enhanced the green of her eyes. The
probationary goodwill now existing between the girls had allowed
Susan to accept the loan of a spangled scarf from Lucy without
feeling patronized.

Lucy's worry about a partner was laid to rest as soon as the sets began to form for the first dance and two pleasant but unremarkable young men presented themselves. Both were known to Mrs Rothwell and Susan, but Lucy heard their names in a daze as she curtsied. The taller young man had turned to Susan and Lucy laid her hand on the arm offered by the other, dazzling him with the smile with which she rewarded him for saving her from the horror of being partnerless.

A second dance followed in the same satisfactory manner and the two girls had just returned to sit beside Mrs Rothwell when the late arrival of three men and a single lady in a stylish rose-coloured gown sent a stir through the room. Mrs Rothwell, on the far side of Susan, was deep in conversation with a friend who had taken a seat next to her. The late-come group had just passed Lucy and the Rothwells when Susan nudged Lucy.

'Those people who just went by – Mrs Hathaway told Mama a moment ago that one of the men is the new owner of your – of Herriards. Mrs Hathaway lives here in Ashwick and she says the fair-haired man is Sir Peter Eddis with whom he is staying at present. The lady is Mrs Lingard, Sir Peter's sister, who is also on a visit to him. The remaining man is her husband.'

Lucy could see only the backs of those in the group now and her gaze blazed across them: two dark-haired men and the fair-haired Sir Peter. . . .' Which is the new owner of Herriards and what is his name?' she demanded fiercely, her memory of a certain caustic voice loud in her ears.

'I don't know and I can't ask because I was not supposed to be listening.'

But now there were two more latecomers walking in their direction: Jane Bellmore and her grandmother, Lady Vauncey. Lucy rose to greet them. Lady Vauncey was slightly in advance of Jane, a tall woman, imposingly gowned, turbaned and bejewelled. It was impossible for her ladyship not to see Lucy, but to her astonishment, the woman's gaze swept over her without the least sign of recognition and without the least check in her progress, forcing Lucy to step back hastily. Jane had been looking towards the centre of the room and saw Lucy only at the last moment. She halted, but before she could speak Lady Vauncey called over her shoulder, 'Come, Jane. Don't dawdle or there will be no chairs for us.'

Jane, flushing as deeply red as Lucy, threw her a look of mingled entreaty and embarrassment and hurried after her grandmother.

Lucy stood as though rooted, her flush fading into the pallor of shock. Slowly she became aware that the first group had turned, was coming towards them and had witnessed that crushing putdown. Lucy flushed anew, wondering if the new owner of Herriards would now add to her embarrassment by recognizing her as his intruder, the *tinker's brat*. The last remnant of her pleasure in the evening faded away.

It was Susan coming to draw her back towards her seat that woke her to the realization that she was attracting notice standing where she was. Before she had taken her seat she found Sir Peter had brought his guests to be introduced to Mrs Hathaway. Introductions to the rectory party followed. Lucy heard the name of the new owner of Herriards with horrified disbelief: Lord Verrell, Baron Farleton.

The man her father had so deeply wronged.

CHAPTER FIVE

In one flying, apprehensive glance, Lucy took in that he was the taller of the two dark-haired men, lean and upright, severe of face, his mouth a forbidding line. Unforgiving, she thought; a face to match the harsh cynicism of the voice she remembered only too well. And this was the man who had bought Herriards, who would live amidst what had once been Daunton possessions. A man who, if he harboured vengeful feelings, she might have reason to fear.

The fact that he had chosen to live in Chalworth, that her home and all that had been her father's property was now his, seemed to her unhappy mind to point in that direction. With her father beyond reach but his daughter close at hand, might he not be tempted to extend his bitterness towards her, even if the intention was not what had brought him here? She had no notion how he might express such bitterness, but alarm whirled in a dark cloud through her mind. Was she never to emerge from the tortuous maze her life had entered?

She heard Mrs Rothwell's voice say, '. . . and this is our young cousin, Miss Daunton . . . Lucy, Lord Verrell.' She sketched an uncertain curtsy, not daring a second look at him.

The meeting was as unexpected to Verrell as it was to Lucy.

43

Daunton's daughter and his own recent prowler. . . . His gaze sharpened to cynical derision. If the girl's downcast gaze was meant to be a show of modesty, it was overdone. Cast in the same deceitful mould as her father, doubtless, and with a moral code as twisted as his.

He became aware that Peter Eddis was looking at him with a slightly mocking lift of his brows and realized he was yielding to rank the choice of which girl to invite to join the dance just forming. He had no wish to dance, no wish to be here at all: he had simply fallen in with a majority vote. His mood soured by the encounter with Miss Daunton, he gave a small shake of his head to indicate that the field was open to Peter to choose. He realized his mistake when Peter walked on to the floor with Miss Rothwell on his arm leaving him with the obligation to invite the other girl to dance. He'd be damned if he would! As though unrealizing, swiftly and adroitly, he involved himself in conversation with the other members of the group.

Watching Susan and Sir Peter on their way to join the dancers, Lucy's heart plummeted. Inevitably, Lord Verrell would now invite her to partner him. She did not think she could endure it.

A minute or two later, she realized his lordship's deep engrossment in the general conversation was to avoid asking her to partner him. Her feelings immediately divided sharply between relief and humiliation at this second snub. The evening was becoming a nightmare.

The first dance of the pair was ending when a voice said, 'Lucy! I have only just learnt you are here.'

She looked up into the smiling blue eyes of Jane Bellmore's brother, Robin. In formal evening dress he looked more handsome than she remembered and his silver-embroidered white waistcoat showed off an equally handsome fob watch.

'Robin! How lovely to see you!' Her delighted smile faded

quickly. 'But should you – I mean Lady Vauncey—' She floundered into silence.

He did not pretend to misunderstand her. 'Yes, Jane told me Grandmama cut you. I'm sorry for it, Lucy, but I ain't under Grandmother's thumb the way Jane is.' His glance took in the older members of her group seemingly absorbed with one another. 'We can join the second dance, if we hurry,' he suggested. 'It's that new thing come over from France, the quadrille. We can talk as we stumble around.'

His cheerful quirkiness lifted her spirits and she laid a hand on his arm with pleasure.

'You're prettier than ever,' Robin bent his curly head to whisper as they walked out to take their places.

Her smile lit her eyes, put dimples in her cheeks. 'And you look very grown up . . . very dashing.'

'Well, it's more than a year since you last saw me and I'm past my twenty-second birthday now,' he said with all the satisfaction of one who has reached the fullness of maturity. His expression became more serious. 'I only heard about – about your father and so on, after my return, Lucy. I'm truly sorry. It must have been a wretched time for you.'

'Yes. But don't let us speak of it now. Tell me about your journeying.'

'Well, I enjoyed most of it, though trotting around the British Isles isn't the same as a Grand Tour through Europe would have been. Still, with Napoleon laid by the heels in St Helena and things fairly settled down, Grandmama says I may yet do the round, but she wants me at home a while first.'

Little more could be said when the dancing began but as they made a dawdling return to Mrs Rothwell, Robin told her, 'Jane was sorry she dared not stop when she first saw you, Lucy, but she is anxious to speak to you. She said she'd slip away from

Grandmama about now and wait for you in what they call the green room. It's at the end of the passage beyond that door over there.' He nodded in the direction he meant.

Mrs Rothwell and Susan were without other company Lucy was relieved to see on reaching them. Introduced, Robin remained as long as politeness required before leaving them and soon after Lucy was able to make an excuse and go to her meeting with Jane.

His sister and her husband having walked on ahead when they parted from the Rothwell group, Sir Peter took advantage of being alone with Harry Verrell to say, 'I was surprised you did not dance with Miss Rothwell's cousin. She looked as charming a little creature as one could wish to meet.'

Verrell's black brows rose. 'Yet you chose to dance with Miss Rothwell.'

'Ah, well—' Sir Peter smiled rather consciously. 'There was a certain meeting of the eyes that somehow decided the matter. But *your* omission had a touch of singularity, the cousin being such a pretty girl.'

'Pretty or not, I found I could not raise the slightest desire to dance with Anthony Daunton's daughter.'

'*Daunton!* Good lord, Harry, her name passed me by. I'd never have left you in such a fix if I'd made the connection. But you know what I am for names.'

'It was no great matter. A pretty little flibbertigibbet like that did not have to wait long before a partner presented himself.'

Sir Peter frowned. 'Bit ungenerous, don't you think, Harry? She's very young and in no enviable situation from what I now recall.'

Verrell's lip curled. 'With such looks as she has, she'll soon find herself a husband.'

46

Sir Peter glanced sideways at his friend, but said nothing.

Conscious of that silence, Verrell said harshly, 'I'm not the man you knew at university, Peter.'

'No,' Peter agreed soberly, 'you're not. Not to be expected.' He let a moment or two pass, then said reflectively, 'I recall now . . . Herriards was Daunton's house, wasn't it? Was there a particular reason you chose to buy it?'

The question flicked Verrell on a sensitive nerve. Venomously, he returned, 'Why do you think? To revenge myself on his daughter? Seduce her? Rape her? Murder her? If so, I don't doubt you will wish to end our acquaintance. You need only say so!'

'Steady, Harry! It was just curiosity. Vulgar, if you like. Consider the question unasked.'

Abruptly, Verrell stopped walking and laid a hand on the other man's arm. 'Good God, Peter, to have spoken so to you! Forgive me. Meeting the girl has thrown me completely off balance. The name *Daunton*—' He shook his head. 'I've lived so long in rough company. I'm not fit for civilized society. I need time by myself to recover some part of the decent manners I once had. I'll rejoin you shortly.' With that, he strode away out of the room.

The only light in the Green Room came from the flare and flicker provided by the leaping flames of the sea-coal fire in the grate. Entering, Lucy found Jane had not yet arrived. Warm from dancing, she did not approach the fire but stood in the shadows, her grey dress making her one with them. Idly she watched the shifting play of light on the polished surfaces of what furniture the room contained. The lilt of a waltz came as a dreamy murmur from afar.

The door opened and she turned expectantly towards it. It was not Jane who entered however, but the person who of all the company she least wished to see.

Lost in thought, it was only after he had closed the door and walked into the centre of room that Verrell caught the muted glimmer of her gown. A moment later he recognized her.

On edge as he was, his first thought was an irritated *Damn the girl!* Seeking solitude, to come again on the very cause of his being off balance and out of temper added fuel to the fire. What the devil was she doing here anyway? His eyes narrowed as what seemed to him the most likely probability sprang into his mind. What else but an assignation with the young sprig who had danced with her? But it was no business of his and convention required him to withdraw and leave her in possession of the room.

But some mischievous imp called up Peter's reminder that she was very young. So she was! Young – and by all appearances in need of schooling.

Harshly, he said, 'Well, Miss Daunton, we meet again.'

Lucy, well taught, recognized his failure to withdraw as a discourtesy. His tone was another and she knew herself to be under attack. With little social experience, she was uncertain how best to defend herself, but managed to say with an appearance of coolness, 'So we do, my lord.'

The coolness misled him. No sense of shame on being discovered, it appeared. A brazen little hussy with no care for her reputation. He stalked towards her.

'I imagine you have not come here in search of solitude. A clandestine meeting with your recent partner, perhaps?'

Lucy's eyes widened at the open sneer, but discovered in that moment a fighting spirit she had not known she possessed. Drawing herself up to the limit of her small height, she returned, 'You may think as you choose, sir, but the reason I am here is my own business and none of yours.'

'True. If it were, you would know the difference between what you should do and what you should not, I assure you.'

Her indignation grew. Grasping at a recollection of Miss Tressick's tone and style when very annoyed, in fair imitation she said, 'Indeed! I can imagine the mode of your instruction and count myself fortunate not to be subject to it.' And was then inspired to pause long enough to give offence before adding, 'My lord!'

A degree of rage entirely irrational roared through Verrell. Reaching out, he gripped her shoulders and dragged her close. 'Perhaps a demonstration of the consequences your kind of behaviour is likely to attract will be more salutary.'

His mouth came down on hers in a kiss that was all punishment. Her shocked lack of defence, or even resistance, fired the first shaft of returning sanity into his brain to warn him of his unreason. In the next instant the door opened again and a girl's voice was saying breathlessly, 'Lucy, are you here? I'm sorry to have kept you— Oh!' The voice broke off in a gasp.

Releasing his captive so suddenly he had to throw a hand to steady her, Verrell glanced from the newcomer to Lucy and back. The full enormity of his behaviour and the mistake he had made hit him like a blow. Appalled, he could find no words adequate to the situation.

The strength of her outrage forced Lucy out of paralysis. Grasping the back of a chair back to give her stability, she looked at Jane standing in the doorway in scandalized amazement, dragged breath into her lungs and said with a force and composure that astonished herself, 'Leave the door open, Jane. This – this *gentleman* is just going.

The general acceptance that a first ball was remembered with pleasure was not true for her, Lucy reflected when she lay in bed that night. All that was most memorable about it was far from pleasant.

Lady Vauncey's public set-down had underlined in a very particular way the difference between Miss Daunton of Herriards and a young woman dependent on rectory charity. But for that to be followed by a first meeting with Lord Verrell, then to be rebuffed by him and finally to suffer his malevolent and insulting assault on her was to fix the occasion in her mind forever as a truly wretched one.

Indignation surged through her anew. *Odious man!* Brutish and coarse-minded! Her enemy indeed! *He* to accuse *her* of impropriety and then to behave towards her as he had!

Jane, always a timid girl, had been almost as deeply shocked as she was – and that merely at walking in on such a scene. Told of the assumptions Lord Verrell had made on the strength of finding Lucy alone in an unlit room, she had been shaken by guilt.

'I should not have asked you to come here. But who could have expected— Oh, Lucy, we shall have to warn people what kind of man he is!'

'How can we if you don't want your grandmother to know of our meeting?'

Jane had looked alarmed. 'Oh, dear! Indeed she must not know! But it seems so wrong that people should not be told.'

'I suspect that many would not care. Because he's a lord. They would prefer to say it was *my* fault,' Lucy said with new-found cynicism.

'Yes. Perhaps you are right. I'm so sorry, Lucy. Sorry about Grandmother, too. She is— She was sure you would have to go for a governess and she said it would not be proper for me to contin—'

Jane hurriedly abandoned that to say, 'The trouble is, when Papa was killed at Talavera, it left Mama, Robin and me very much dependent on her, so we have to follow her wishes. You know what a sad invalid Mama is. She gets very upset if

Grandmama is put out in any way, so we, Robin and I, have to
be careful. Of course, Robin being a man does rather more as he
pleases. But there are limits to what even he can do.'

Robin . . . Lucy turned to the only truly pleasant moments of the
evening. Not only was he someone from her past, but he had
defied his grandmother to dance twice with her. He had behaved
charmingly, too. More so than he had before he had started out
on his journeying, when she and Jane, both sixteen, had giggled
over his awkward compliments to Lucy. Since then, some of his
time had been spent in London where his manners had acquired
a certain gloss and he had learned how to make himself agreeable to others.

Considering her other partners of this evening, she realized
that pleasant young men though they had been, no one of standing had invited her to dance. As the penniless daughter of a
bankrupt suspected of suicide she was now all but invisible to society.

'If a matter is beyond alteration do not waste time and
energy repining,' she remembered Miss Tressick's repeated
advice. 'Apply your intelligence to the situation and make the
best you can of it.'

Once she had thought it mere prosing, but she saw its point
and value now. She had drifted through the past months, accepting decisions made for her by others, still thinking only vaguely of
how to support herself. It was time for action. If she was destined
to become a governess, the sooner she started out on her career
the better. What she could not do was remain forever dependent
on the Rothwells.

Marrying Robin would be happier option, if Robin had that in
mind, but it was more than likely that Lady Vauncey would throw
a rub in the way of it. She sighed. There was little to charm her

in the idea of becoming a governess and she wondered now what Miss Tressick had thought and felt about her life at Herriards. She found herself wishing she had behaved with more thoughtfulness towards her. Yet the poor woman had been in a flood of tears when they had said goodbye, so perhaps she had not been the worst pupil ever . . . .

CHAPTER SIX

Four days after the ball at Ashwick, Chalworth was buzzing with the news that the new owner of Herriards had taken up residence there. Three days later the new owner waited in the room he was using as a temporary office for Penfold to bring the rector to him.

Matthew Rothwell was the only visitor Verrell was prepared to receive. Following the events of the ball, he had been glad when his visit to Peter Eddis reached its end. His years in exile, he had decided, had made him unfit for English society. At Herriards he could shut himself up, be at home to no one and earn a reputation for being a recluse if he chose. The rector had to be excepted.

Suspecting that welcoming a new parishioner was not the reason – or not the only reason – for the man's visit, he would not, for pride's sake, attempt to avoid it.

He was not proud of his behaviour at the Ashwick ball. Starting with his odiously offensive rejection of Peter's quiet enquiry regarding his purchase of Herriards, he had gone on to make unjustifiable assumptions concerning Lucy Daunton's character and then to manhandle her. Having taken the girl into his care, the rector had a legitimate complaint against him.

Honesty required him to accept that there were forces in him

that he had failed to recognize and now could not ignore. All too
close to the surface there lay a smoking anger that volcano-like,
burst from him in small fumaroles on slight provocation. '*Take
care*,' Louise had warned him: he should have given more heed
to her words. As it was, he would now have to endure being
taken to task by a country parson, if the man so chose. On the
other hand, he might prove chicken-hearted and dodge the issue.
He smiled grimly.

He had been looking through the maps and deeds of his new
property when Penfold had brought the rector's card to him.
Hearing footsteps approaching now, he stood up and came out
from behind the littered table at which he had been working.

The door opened and Penfold, uneasy in his new role of butler,
made unpolished work of announcing the visitor.

Waiting to see what manner of man his visitor was, Verrell did
not immediately step forward to welcome him when he entered.
The first sharp glance told him that this was neither an unworldly
innocent, nor a man likely to dodge any issue in which he had an
interest. A match for his own height, he judged, and a figure that
showed little difference from what it must have been in athletic
youth. His gaze was caught and held by one as long and keen as
his own and knew himself to be as much under judgement as was
his visitor.

It was the uncommon charm of the rector's smile however, that
impelled Verrell forward with his hand outstretched. When they
were both seated, recognizing the kind of papers that had been
engaging Verrell's attention, Matthew made some slight remark
regarding them which led easily into a discussion of Chalworth
and its affairs generally. Little by little the conversation expanded
to embrace larger subjects and the visit lengthened beyond either
man's expectation. It had not taken long for Verrell to decide that
Miss Daunton had told no tales and by the time the rector rose to

go, he knew himself to be indebted to the girl for her reticence whatever her reason for it might be. That Matthew Rothwell was a man of strong character and considerable intelligence was easily recognized: he was also, Verrell thought, a man whose good opinion was to be valued.

Reporting his visit to those gathered round the rectory dinner-table that evening, the rector told them that though he had found Lord Verrell stiff and remote to begin with, when he unbent, he had proved to be a sensible man of wide and interesting experience. Mrs Rothwell, when she had mentioned her meeting with his lordship at the ball, pronounced him cold and severe. Remembering this, Matthew Rothwell looked at her and added, 'He takes a while to thaw, as I said, but when he does, he's worth talking to.' He twinkled a smile at her. 'He knows his Virgil and his Horace, though the machinery of memory creaked a little from disuse.'

Familiar with her husband's bias, Mrs Rothwell laughed. 'He can need no further recommendation then, can he?'

Though the rector's smile deepened, he had no more to say regarding Lord Verrell at that time.

Lucy, with her own much less favourable opinion of his lordship, said nothing at all, but the following day she spoke to Mrs Rothwell regarding her intention to look for a position as a governess and asked how to set about it. Such a position would, she hoped, put her at a distance from the man who, by the evidence, regarded her as an enemy.

Mrs Rothwell was doubtful of the project. 'I think you will need to wait a year or so before you can hope for employment of any kind,' she told her gently.

'But why? Miss Tressick thought me a good scholar and I know we covered more subjects than do many girls. And I had masters for painting and the pianoforte, too.'

Mrs Rothwell looked at her and sighed. 'Your scholarship is not the problem: it is your youth. Ladies generally prefer someone a little older to take their children in charge.' *And regard prettiness in a governess as undesirable*, she thought, but did not say.

'Then perhaps I could be a companion to an elderly lady, or an invalid. Someone of that sort.'

'Yes, perhaps. But such positions do not abound,' Mrs Rothwell conceded doubtfully. 'Are you so very anxious to leave us? We are in no hurry for you to go.'

'But I am an expense to you and I have no right to be. Might not Mr Rothwell have heard of someone in need of a companion?'

'He has not mentioned anyone having such a need, but I will ask him.' She shook her head at the girl. 'Do not think of yourself as a burden to us, Lucy. For my part, I should like you to be content to remain with us a year or two more, during which time it is not at all unlikely that you might attach a gentleman who would wish to marry you. That is surely to be preferred to your being confined to a schoolroom or sick-room?'

There was no time to discuss this because Jessie came in to announce the arrival of Sir Peter Eddis and his sister, Mrs Lingard.

It being a first visit, the brother and sister remained no more than half an hour, but before it ended, Lucy noticed, Sir Peter made opportunity to move his seat close to Susan and engage her in conversation. Susan's colour rose, but otherwise she received the attention with composure.

Hardly had these visitors left them when, to Lucy's surprise and pleasure, Robin and Jane rode in. After ten minutes of polite conversation, Mrs Rothwell said with an understanding smile, 'The weather is so fine and warm still, would not you young people like to walk in the garden?'

The suggestion was adopted with relief and the four were released into the sunshine and a less formal atmosphere.

'We must not stay too long,' Jane whispered worriedly, as they went two and two down one of the narrower paths. 'Robin *would* come, but Grandmama does not know of it and will ask questions if we are away too long.'

Soon Robin changed places with his sister and Lucy had the pleasure of chatting over old times and laughing at remembered foolishness. Then, more seriously, Robin asked, 'Are you happy here, Lucy?'

'I ought to be. Everyone is very kind, but—' The sentence died on a sigh. 'Until I left Herriards I did not realize just how I loved the place. It was my particular Eden, though I wasn't aware of it until I lost it.'

'Yes. Well . . .' Robin said a trifle awkwardly. 'You must find things very different, of course.'

'Yes. But that was not quite what I meant.' She saw his incomprehension and hastily changed the subject. 'Come and look at the pond. Mr Rothwell is very proud of his golden carp.'

When Robin at last paid heed to Jane's worried reminders that they must go home soon, they returned to the house to take leave of Mrs Rothwell before going to the stable yard for the visitors' mounts. Lucy and Susan stood in the lane to wave the pair goodbye and when they re-entered the stable yard, Simon was leading a good-looking clouded grey horse through from the front of the house. 'Whose is that?' Susan asked the boy. 'I don't recognize it.'

' 'Tis Lord Verrell's, miss. Come to see the rector, so I heard him tell Jessie. He's as prime and handsome a fellow as ever I did see, isn't he, miss?'

It took Lucy a startled moment to realize Simon meant the

horse not the man. With no wish for another meeting with his lordship, she tugged at Susan's sleeve 'Shall we stay in the garden a little longer? If his lordship's call is to your father we will not be expected to appear and it is so very pleasant here.'

Knowing nothing of Lucy's encounter with Lord Verrell at the ball, Susan was unsuspicious and readily agreed. 'In any case, Mama will send for us should we be wanted,' she said.

They linked arms and walked to where a bench was set in the dappled shade of a maple and sat there idly chatting for some time before deciding to go and look for windfalls under the late-bearing apple trees. Before they reached the small orchard, a large black shape came hurtling over a little picket side-gate and lolloped towards them, a broken length of cord trailing from its collar.

Susan came to a halt with a horrified gasp. 'A *dog*!' She exclaimed. 'Lucy, I can't – *I can't—*' She turned and bolted towards the house.

The dog stopped a yard or two away with something comically close to a look of surprise on his face, his head swinging between Lucy and the fleeing girl as though undecided whether to give chase or not.

Looking at the animal, huge, powerful and all black except for some tan markings about its broad head, for a moment Lucy was tempted to follow Susan. This, she guessed, was the Juba of her downfall at Herriards and the trailing cord suggested his being here was unauthorized. She was not nervous of dogs; there had been guard dogs for the Herriards' stables and outhouses and she had her own much-loved greyhound named Star, who had lived to be thirteen, dying quietly in her sleep, two years ago. This animal of intimidating size was an un- known quantity, but it seemed important that he should not be allowed to chase the already panic-stricken Susan. She took two steps towards him, which was enough to fix his attention on her.

'Juba,' she called, more in hope than with any confidence and extended a hand towards him.

His head on one side, he padded towards her with cheerful expectancy, sniffed perfunctorily at her fingers, decided they were those of a friend, and licked them with enthusiasm. When Lucy transferred her hand to his head, he further demonstrated his pacific intentions by rearing up to plant two large front paws on her shoulders and salute her face. She staggered back under his weight and excess of cordiality and almost fell.

Moments later, from somewhere behind them a furious voice thundered, 'Down, Juba, damn you! Down, I say!'

Verrell's return visit to Matthew Rothwell had been intended as nothing more than a courtesy call, but again he found himself held by the pleasure of the man's conversation and an increased awareness of how well he liked him.

Sitting in the rector's study, he had a partial view of the garden through its window. Lucy's unsteady backward steps under Juba's friendly assault brought her suddenly into his line of vision. With a vexed exclamation, he leapt to his feet, exclaiming, 'My damned dog is molesting your protégée! Pardon my language, Rector, but would you point me the quickest way to go to her rescue.'

Juba had instantly complied with the angry command and Lucy turned to see Juba's owner bearing down on them. *Like the wrath of God*, she thought, and felt a stronger impulse to retreat before the man than she had before his dog. Perhaps Juba shared something of her feeling, for he leaned his weight against her legs as though in need of reassurance. Lucy rested a comforting hand on the dog's large head.

Striding swiftly towards them across a stretch of lawn, Verrell had a sudden impression of the two being united in defence against him and slackened his pace. Reaching them, he said, 'I apologize for Juba's bad manners, Miss Daunton,' annoyance bristling in his voice.

Suspecting his displeasure was as much with her as with his dog, Lucy returned stiffly, 'He intended no harm and has done none, sir.'

'Perhaps not. But he has no right to be here. He probably alarmed you to begin with. He is very large.'

'No, he did not frighten me,' she said, not quite truthfully, and with a glint in her eyes suggesting Juba's master had recently alarmed her rather more.

All too sensitive on the point, Verrell caught the reminder and turned his irritation on his dog. 'You, sir, have much to learn. You deserve a good thrashing!

Lucy glared at him. 'Oh, do not! He is little more than a pup. He meant only to be friendly.'

It was mortifying to reflect that she had good reason to think him a bully capable of wreaking dreadful punishment on the confounded animal. Memory obligingly recalled her words and tone when she had told him '*I can imagine the mode of your instruction, sir!*' And that was *before* he had inflicted that savage kiss on her.

'I said *deserve*, Miss Daunton, *not* that I would administer it. For his own sake it is necessary for him to learn good behaviour.' Another revealing gleam came into the expressive brown eyes to inform him that she thought Juba's master in greater need of that particular lesson.

The sooner this meeting ended the better, he thought, and picked up the trailing cord attached to the dog's collar. His uneasy conscience however, would not allow him to ignore the fact that he owed her an apology for what had happened at that disastrous first meeting. Much as he would like to bury its memory under a handy mountain, something must be said about it.

The words came dourly. 'I am aware my own behaviour when we last met does not bear examination. It was beyond excuse, so I will attempt none. All I can do is apologize for it.'

Lucy blushed scarlet. Convinced of his all-embracing arrogance, she had expected no such acknowledgment from him. Though she inclined her head in response, she could think of nothing to say . . . not even something she would like to say but must not.

Perhaps because the apology had not been without cost, he had expected more from her and there was an awkward little silence. To break it, he said, 'May I hope that you will be able to put that particular occasion sufficiently out of your mind, so that when we chance to meet we may do so with common civility?' The moment the words were said, he knew he had made another mistake.

The colour that had begun to recede from Lucy's cheeks flooded up again. She heard his words as a warning against making vulgar scenes in public. Resentment loosened her tongue and she answered with angry pride, 'You may rely on it, sir.'

The sharp little voice underlined his error. He was doomed to misjudgement whenever they met, it seemed. *Could* there be a safe meeting-ground anywhere for two people placed as they were? To say anything more at this moment would probably only make matters worse. There was nothing to do but to bow and leave her.

Towed behind his master, aware he was in disgrace, Juba looked back ruefully at the sympathetic presence he was leaving.

Taking refuge in the bedroom, Lucy brooded over Lord Verrell's determination to think her an ill-bred hoyden in need of constant correction.

She could be thankful that their 'chance' meetings were likely to be few. After church on Sundays, possibly, if he ever attended which he had not done so far.

She suspected that his apology had been a heavy charge upon his pride. He deserved no less! She might have valued it more if he had not gone on from there. She understood the reason for his ill-will towards her but it did not make it easier to bear. And she feared she might yet suffer worse from it. Was it Bacon who named revenge a kind of wild justice? As the blameless victim, she could see no justice in it.

'Here you are!' Susan had come into the room. 'Oh, Lucy! What must you think of me running off as I did and leaving you to face that great beast of a dog alone?'

The two girls had been groping towards a renewal of their old fellowship during the past weeks and Susan crossed the room to sit on the bed beside Lucy and slide an arm about her waist.

'You may not have heard, or perhaps you don't remember, that I was bitten by a dog when I was four years old. I have been terrified of them ever since. Especially if they are large and black, as that one was. And never before have I seen such as great dog as that in Chalworth. Nor its kind.'

Lucy grimaced sympathetically. 'He is rather alarming to look at. He is the one I encountered at Herriards and belongs to Lord Verrell. I think he had broken out from somewhere to follow his master today. His name's Juba. He's not very old and really quite friendly. It's his size that makes him so intimidating.'

'Well, if Lord Verrell comes here again I hope he will see his dog is safely held at home.'

Though she did not say so, if either were to come again, Lucy would prefer it should be the dog rather than the man.

CHAPTER SEVEN

Chalworth heard with rejoicing that the disgraceful hovels in Slippy-Slosh Lane were to be pulled down and their inhabitants rehoused in new cottages to be built on drier ground. Work would not begin until the spring, but temporary repairs were already in hand to make roofs watertight, plug gaps around doors and such windows as there were and make some improvement to the sanitary arrangements of the six dwellings for the time they remained occupied.

Slippy-Slosh had once borne another name, but the one it bore now had fitted it so well and for so long, few remembered what the old name had been. The rector was among the first to know of the improvements. Calling on a sick woman who lived in one of the condemned cottages, he came across the architect summoned from Tilchester to draw up plans for the replacements. The man was taking a close look at what his designs were to improve on and expressed the view that just being *new* would be a large improvement, but that he hoped to go well beyond that.

On returning home, the rector told Lucy what was proposed rather than allowing her to hear it first from anyone else.

Profoundly thankful as he was for the proposed change, he softened as far as possible the comparison that inevitably would be made, saying, 'It is fortunate that Lord Verrell's fortune is sufficient to enable him to replace those ancient buildings. It is a prudent step, of course, because in time, it will benefit the estate as a whole.'

Lucy felt colour mount into her cheeks, though it was less for the comparison between her father's attitude to the village and Verrell's than her memory that it had been their visit to the Slippy-Slosh cottages that had set off her quarrel with Susan.

Less pleasing to Chalworth society was his lordship's determined reclusiveness. It was sheer provocation to have a man, young, rich, titled and a bachelor living in their midst but completely inaccessible to ladies with unmarried daughters because there was no lady at Herriards on whom they might call. But it was not only the ladies who had difficulty in making contact with the new owner of Herriards. The rector was the only gentleman known to have been received by Lord Verrell. Others calling were less fortunate: the message – always given with great courtesy – was that that his lordship was *not at home*.

More mindful of her social obligations, Mrs Rothwell was prompt in returning Sir Peter and Mrs Lingard's visit. Lucy and Susan accompanied her and they were fortunate to find Sir Peter sitting with his sister and her husband. Susan again had the felicity of receiving distinguishing notice from him and left Ashwick in a quiet glow, hugging the privately given information that in a week or two's time, when his sister and her husband left him, he expected to be at Herriards for a while to put in some rough shooting. Mrs Rothwell, a quiet observer of the harmony between the two, allowed herself a pleasurable hope, but said nothing to anyone.

The weather continued mild and settled, Robin and Jane Bellmore came to the rectory twice more though their visits never extended much beyond half an hour. Robin made plain his discontent with this brevity, which was due to Jane's nervous fear of their grandmother discovering their destination.

Following the latest visit, when Susan and Lucy were alone in their bedroom, Susan said, 'Jane seems always so afraid of over-staying and incurring her grandmother's anger by it. Yet Robin appears to have no such worry.'

Lucy explained something of the Bellmores' difficult circumstances, ending, 'I think Mrs Bellmore is as nervous of her mother as is Jane. Robin says it has to do with Lady Vauncey not having wished her daughter to marry their father. He says, too, that if his mother and Jane would stand up to Lady Vauncey she would be less tyrannical. But Mrs Bellmore is never really well and Jane has always been timorous. On the other hand, Jane hints that Robin is not quite so free to please himself as he likes to represent.'

'I see that it must be very difficult for them all. I suppose Lady Vauncey has not actually forbidden Robin and Jane to come here? I mean, it would not be right for them to do so if there is an outright ban on it, would it?'

'No. That is precisely why Jane is so anxious to avoid bringing their visits to Lady Vauncey's notice. Perhaps it is not right to deceive by omission, but what harm is being done? Robin and Jane have been my friends for a number of years and not long ago Lady Vauncey welcomed me as a visitor to her home. I have done nothing to deserve her coldness except to have – to have—' She broke off with a shake of her head unable to finish.

Susan gave Lucy's hand a sympathetic squeeze and said no more.

The following day was exceptionally fine and warm for late September. Susan had accompanied her mother to the dentist in Tilchester and Lucy took herself off for a walk through the nearby Chalworth woods. They were part of the Herriards' estate, but there were several footpaths through them that were open to the public. Lucy chose one that led to a swift little brook and followed its course for a while. Coming to a small glade where the brook widened and rippled pleasantly over a lip of rock, she sat down on the bank and gave herself up to a daydream.

She was aware that it was through Robin's insistence that the two Bellmores visited her; Jane was too fearful of her grandmother's discovering them to be happy about coming. Lucy could not help wondering if more than friendship underlay Robin's constancy. Might he eventually make her an offer of marriage? He had said nothing positive yet, but his manner towards her was growing warmer and he made hints that pointed to it. And once, when Jane was not looking, he had ventured to kiss her cheek.

He was a pleasant and good-looking young man, an amusing companion whom she had known for a long time. He was of age and had assured her more than once that he was well able to handle his grandmother. But what of her own feelings?

She liked him, she knew, but she could not say she was in love with him. Nor could she say she was not. Warm feelings in a properly brought up young woman, came *after* marriage, Miss Tressick had told her. With no relative to assume control over her, whom she married was now for her to decide and marriage to Robin was not an unpleasing prospect. Moreover, she knew it to be both suitable and sensible. That it was necessary for her to be sensible on her own behalf, she also knew, because opportunities for her to marry at her own social level were likely to be few. If indeed there were any at all.

Her thoughts were given no chance to go any further: a sudden rush and she was knocked flat by a large, black and very wet shape instantly recognizable as Juba. Pinning her to the ground by standing on her skirt, he tried to lick her face with his usual friendly enthusiasm, dripping a generous share of brook water over her while doing so.

She was pushing vainly against his heavy body when he was suddenly hauled away and an angry voice said, 'Damn you, dog! You're an affliction of the worst kind!'

Released, Lucy sat up. Muddy paw marks and several damp patches decorated the skirt of her lavender-coloured gown. Her villager hat had been knocked from her head and now hung from its ribbons around her neck and adding to her sense of injury, Lord Verrell stood looking down at her with scowling impatience as though *she* were the one at fault.

'Allow me to help you up,' he said shortly.

Annoyed, but feeling obliged to accept the hand he held out her, she allowed him to help her to her feet. She thanked him with chilly gratitude.

Watching her unknot the ribbons of her hat with sharp little tugs indicative of a quite justifiable vexation, Verrell forced himself into further speech. 'Once again I must apologize for Juba's behaviour. I cannot think what it is about you that impels him to persecute you with his attentions. You are the only person to whom he behaves so.'

The terse tone of his apology annoyed her still more and forgetting caution, she gave him a glittering glance and said, 'Thank you, sir. It is a great comfort to me to know that.'

Had his apology sounded churlish? Perhaps it had. Because of the recurrence of his need to make her one. And perhaps because of whom she was. He wished he could forget it; forget her existence. It was ironic that though he successfully avoided meeting others when he so chose, malign circumstances too often thrust a meeting with Miss Daunton on him. What was worse, he seemed never to emerge from them without damage to his self-esteem. Another vexation was that having dismissed her as of little account, little by little he was being forced to recognize a sharper intelligence and a livelier personality behind the pretty face than it pleased him to find. Nor was he blind to the occasional flicker of apprehension in her eyes when he came on her unawares. Clearly, she expected no good of him. And why should she?

Coolly, he said, 'My apology was sincere. With the evidence before me of the havoc wrought by my wretched hound I am conscious of how much at fault he is.'

She inclined her head but did not speak.

He frowned, found something to carp at and said sharply, 'Should you be here alone? I understand there are tinkers in Pilgrim's Dingle, which is not very far from here.'

Reminded of his first estimation of her as a *tinker's brat*, Lucy said a little too quickly, 'They will be Aaron Smiths'. They are Romanies, not tinkers, and have permission.' She flushed. 'I mean, in the past they were given permission. They come to Chalworth each year about this time and are quite respectable in their way. I sometimes played with the children when I was young.'

Young! He almost laughed. What did she think she was now? He was not willing to yield ground, though. 'There are other dangers than gypsies. I cannot think it is wise for you to be here without a companion. I trust you will accept my escort back to the rectory.'

The way her head lifted at times was becoming familiar to him.

'It is quite unnecessary. I have walked these woods as long as I can remember. What danger can there be in this small village?' She skimmed past the fact that she had not been allowed to walk alone if Miss Tressick knew her intention.

Opposition put a glint in his eyes. 'Something tells me, Miss Daunton, that you are more annoyed with me than my offending dog.'

'Rightly so, if I am. You, sir, are the intelligent being in authority over him.' It always surprised her how readily the words to keep him at bay came to her. She was thankful for it, for she had no other weapon with which to oppose him and she had not the least doubt that they were in opposition to one another.

He smiled at her, a sleek, unkind smile. 'I wish you will inform Juba. He is far from persuaded it is so.'

'Perhaps because he has the greater—' She broke off, flushing scarlet. That was to go too far! Her annoyance with him was tripping her into being as unpardonably pert as the ill-bred creature he already thought her.

'—the greater intelligence,' he finished for her with an unkindness to match his smile. 'Yes, there is that possibility.'

'I beg your pardon. I did not mean to be impertinent. I should not have said—' She bit her lip.

'But you did not . . . quite.' He glanced at her down bent head, and surprising himself as much as her, this time he did laugh. 'Don't take it to heart, Miss Daunton. Worse things have been said of me and to me. And Juba, despite his lack of discipline, is very intelligent. But who knows – one day I may catch up with him.'

Trying to bring their exchange on to a more normal level, she asked hurriedly, 'What kind is he? He is not of a sort commonly seen.'

'I do not know, though I am told he has some resemblance to

a breed they have in Germany, but is overlarge to be pure bred. I found him wandering in a war-shattered village in France early this year. Possibly the unsanctioned offspring of a dog accompanying the German troops. He was no more than a lost and hungry pup, half the size he is now.'

Without Lucy realizing it, they had begun walking back along the path by which she had come. Watching the huge dog padding along ahead of them, she said, 'And still a pup! You named him well. Black and princely and, I imagine, loyal.'

'His loyalty has yet to be tested,' Verrell said drily. And then, more fully realizing what she had said, he turned a surprised look on her. 'You know the source of Juba's name? Are acquainted with Addison's *Cato?*'

'Yes.'

His expressive eyebrows arched. 'You surprise me again, Miss Daunton.'

She threw him a sharp glance. 'If that is to infer there is a wonder in my having read Addison, the credit must go to Miss Tressick, my governess.'

'So . . . she has made a budding blue-stocking of you.'

'Another mark against me, I must suppose,' she returned, with something close to a snap.

'Now why should you think so?'

She gave him look for look, good resolutions forgotten. 'Most girls are informed early that to be dubbed a bluestocking by a gentleman is uncomplimentary. Gentlemen, we learn, prefer ladies to be witless and uneducated except in the entertaining arts.'

Miss Tressick should have warned her against such devastating candour, he thought. 'It is not a preference I entertain, I assure you. But why should I hold *any* marks against you?'

'That you do has been clear to me since we first met. The

greatest one I cannot escape: I cannot refute the charge of being my father's daughter.'

Again straight to the point and spoken in a tone that said clearly she would make no apology for it. He was silenced. It was a fact. She was her father's daughter. It lay between them like a sword.

A few paces more and they came to the edge of the wood and stepped out into the lane. Both busy with their own thoughts, their silence held over the next fifty yards before they turned into the village street. Verrell glanced at his companion's face. She looked unhappy. He felt a stab of guilt but quickly rejected it. Who she was was not her fault, but it could not be changed.

Here at the southern end of Chalworth, they were nearer the rectory than Herriards and, reaching the rectory gate, Verrell broke the silence to say in a cold and distant tone faintly tinged with sarcasm, aimed as much at himself as at her, 'You see you have returned in my company at least as well as you might have done without it. Having Juba, I will come no further. The rector explained Miss Rothwell's terror of dogs to me. Will you say what is proper for me?'

She turned towards him, her dark gaze lifting to meet his, her expression very sober. 'It was good of you to come out of your way, sir. I am conscious of having spoken several times as I think I should not have done. I beg your pardon.'

'You have said nothing I have not provoked . . . nothing I shall remember. But for my dog's misdemeanours, you have my sincere apologies.'

As she passed in through the gate he held open for her something prompted him to add, 'I shall study to match Juba's intelligence.'

Hurrying to the door of the house, Lucy was uncertain whether he had spoken sarcastically or had made a small joke. She wondered why he had insisted on accompanying her back to the rectory. She was fairly certain the answer to that was because she had resisted it.

Verrell, walking down the street at a speed that defied inter-ruption, asked himself the same question and came to the same conclusion.

CHAPTER EIGHT

Jane was in a markedly querulous mood when next she and Robin came to visit Lucy. Because Robin had coerced her into keeping her promise to accompany him, she had been obliged to hold out against her grandmother's wish for her company, much to that lady's annoyance.

The late October day was fine enough for a stroll in the woods to be decided on and Robin and the three girls set out, Jane looping her riding-skirt over her arm. When Jane and Susan were out of earshot, Robin said, 'I imagine Jane has been complaining of being ill used? The thing is, I *had* to see you today because I'm off in a day or two to stay with a friend in Wiltshire for a month and maybe more. Grandmama has invited an unknown female to stay for two or three weeks, a Miss Broderick. Luckily I got wind of it and was able to persuade my friend to write pressing me for an immediate visit. Else I'd have been roped in to squire the unknown around.'

With no more than a pause for breath, he went on, 'I suspect the old lady of having wedding-bells in mind. Miss Broderick, it appears, is an heiress, but with twenty-six years in her dish and still unwed, she's probably at her last prayers and muffin-faced into the bargain. My going away put the old lady out of frame, of course, but Freddie being the second son of a marquis sweetened the pill.'

Something about this speech made Lucy uncomfortable, but before she could give it any thought, Robin had drawn her to a halt. With a quick glance at the two girls walking ahead of them, he put his hands on her shoulders and smiling down into her eyes, said softly, 'It may be past Christmas before I see you again, Lucy . . . will you miss me?'

She gave him a sparkling look. 'As much as you will miss me while you are shooting over your friend's coverts, fishing his lakes or rivers, or riding his splendid acres. I assume he is able to offer these entertainments as the second son of a marquis still living at home?'

'Well, yes, he has. But they won't stop me thinking of you.'

Still teasing, she said, 'Well *I* might be thinking of *him* and those acres! Perhaps you'll bring him home with you? Introduce me. He's still a bachelor, I imagine.'

'Lucy, you little wretch! I wouldn't let him anywhere near you, you're much too pretty!' With another glance along the now empty path, he slid his arms round her and drawing her close, pressed his lips to hers.

'*There*! Perhaps that will help to keep me in mind and stop you thinking about the son of a marquis and his father's marquisorial property.'

It was the first time he had kissed her on the lips. His mouth had been soft and eager, offering nothing resembling the savage assault of Lord Verrell's. Certainly she found nothing in it to appal her as his lordship's had. What surprised her was that something so rigorously forbidden could prove so unexciting.

Later, when Jane and Robin had gone, her thoughts returned to the slight discomfort she had felt at Robin's determined avoidance of his grandmother's guest. She recognized that the

Bellmore dependency on Lady Vauncey placed them in a difficult position, and it was not surprising if Robin, expecting all the freedom usually allowed the young male, chafed at any restriction placed on him. Yet in many ways, Lady Vauncey treated him with great indulgence. To escort her guest about for a few weeks did not seem a great deal to ask in return. No one could make him propose to Miss Broderick if he did not choose to do so.

But who was she to judge him? Her own behaviour in acquiescing in keeping Lady Vauncey in ignorance of Jane and Robin's visits to her was not above reproach. There was, she knew, something of self-interest in it. Both were familiar and dear to her but, she suspected, Robin was her only hope for marriage with an equal. She had to think for herself now and look at such things as a parent might, which meant taking thought for the future and approaching the possibility of marriage in a well-judging and prudent way. She sighed. Somehow such practical considerations robbed the prospect of all romance.

By the end of October, Verrell found himself with time of his hands. Everything that could be done to put the neglected Herriards estate on the way to improvement and profitability this side of winter had been done or begun. He began now to miss the everyday cut and thrust of the businesses he had built up in Burma and India and elsewhere and the many and diverse people he met through them. His dealings in jade, emeralds and silk had brought him into contact with men of every sort and many nationalities. Honest men and rogues; men with high intelligence and others with low cunning. Experience had honed his own intelligence, sharpened his native wits and given him friends among both the good and the bad. The lessons he had learned through them had contributed largely to the changes worked in him: he could never now be the Harrington Verrell he would have been if he had never left England. For good or ill, Adam Lang was an inescapable *alter ego*.

Peter Eddis's visit to Herriards had been deferred because of a death in his family, which meant that Verrell had nothing in prospect now but his own company until some time after Christmas.

His mind turned to the Reverend Rothwell. *There* was a man whose acquaintance it would be a pleasure to cultivate. The drawback to it was the presence of Lucy Daunton in the rector's home. She was a constant reminder of her father and he had reached a state of mind where he would be glad to forget them both. A little thought brought him to the conclusion that a chatelaine at Herriards would provide a buffer between himself and the ladies of the rector's household and reduce the irritant.

He wrote at once to his sister, to ask if Louise knew of and could recommend any particular one among their unattached aunts and older cousins who might be willing to undertake the role of hostess for him. She replied promptly that Julia Gresham, their mother's elder sister, living in Hampshire in somewhat straitened circumstances was the most likely and would probably prove the most congenial candidate.

He had a distant memory of a pleasant, lively, sophisticated woman and two days later, rode into Hampshire to renew his acquaintance with her. He found her very much as he remembered her. She had always been handsome rather than pretty and though time had taken toll, she was, in her fifty-eighth year, still an attractive woman. Inescapably, past events were discussed.

'I did not see you often as a young man,' she told him, 'but I remember you well enough to know that I liked what I saw in you. Living in Sussex as I did at the time, I knew nothing of Lorimer's murder until after you had left the country. Naturally, I was shocked. I would never have suspected you of having a violent temper, but there was talk of a drunken brawl between two young men. In such circumstances one supposes anything might happen. I wondered about you, what you were doing cut off from your family and adrift in a hard world. But chiefly, I think, I was thankful your mother did not have to face the terrible shock and grief of it all.'

She gave Verrell a sideways smile. 'Your disappearing was the best thing you could have done as things have turned out . . . for yourself, as it now appears, and for the family at the time. Louise writes to me quite frequently. She told me of your visit and that you were bitter at finding Daunton, his brother and your father all dead. It must have been a grief to you not to see your father again.'

After a pause, he said, 'I was past feeling grief by the time I learned of his death. It was more a vexation, a frustration, that I could not bring him to acknowledge he was wrong to have believed me guilty. He, of all people, should surely have known me.'

Mrs Gresham regarded the unyielding expression on her nephew's dark face and wondered how much of the younger Harry remained in the present one – if indeed anything did. She said, 'Twelve years . . . a long time, Harry. Were there no gains?'

He smiled thinly. 'Materially, yes. A fortune in fact and I still own two of its sources. Add to that a world of experience I would not otherwise have had. But all gained at cost, my dear aunt. To the spirit, to character.'

'Are there things you are ashamed to have done?'

He turned his thoughts inward for a moment. Then he said slowly, 'There are things I wish I had not done . . . had not *had* to do. But ashamed? No. But I can only hope I did not sink so low that I should have been.'

'Then it is time to forget. And possibly forgive.'

78

'Neither easy. Perhaps if I could have met Anthony Daunton again – I came back for justice. Or so I thought. Yet, when I found it had already been granted it did not satisfy me. Perhaps I wanted revenge. I don't know.'

'Revenge? Oh no! Not you, Harry. I cannot believe you are that much changed.'

He gave her a curious look. 'Touching faith, my dear aunt, but the early years were hard enough to make it unsurprising if I wanted something out of Anthony Daunton's hide.'

The marks of that hardship showed in the lines in his face. She said briskly, 'Well, he's beyond your reach, so stop looking back. Here you are, thirty-four years old, with your reputation restored, obviously healthy, and you say, wealthy. That makes you more fortunate than many men. You have reason enough to begin to enjoy life now.' She leaned back in her chair, her smile warming on him. 'You have asked me to be your hostess . . . a wife would meet your need better. Have you had no thought of acquiring one?'

'I have had more important things to think of.'

She laughed. 'Such arrogance. You cannot mean it!'

He had meant it, though he had spoken carelessly. Startled, he asked, 'Arrogance?'

Again she looked at him consideringly. 'I leave it with you to think about,' she said finally and though she still smiled, her eyes were troubled. Perhaps he was right about the cost to his character – what did she know of the present Harry Verrell? Was she wise to consider giving up her independence – poor though it was – to take charge of the household of a man with such stringent views? The doubt unresolved, she said, 'I shall not be sorry to leave these cramped quarters and as there is a ready market for cheap accommodation, this house will be easy to rent out. I should be free to come to you by Christmas, if that will suit you?

There is, however, one thing I ask of you. . . .'

'Which is?'

'Call me what you choose when we are in company, but Julia is what I would prefer when we are just two together.'

'Julia it shall be, Aunt.' The unexpected, teasing warmth of his smile put something back in his face that made him more recognizably the easy-going young man she had known.

Though Susan had indicated she was free to make use of the piano whenever she chose, Lucy was cautious in doing so. Without vanity, she was aware of the superiority of her own playing to Susan's and she was reluctant to make any display of the difference. But whenever chance took all the Rothwells out of the house at the same time, she seized the opportunity to indulge herself to the full.

One day, having such a chance, she concentrated first on recovering her fingers' dexterity, but after a time turned to trying out the last piece she had been working on under Professor Lowson's guidance.

Having decided to further his acquaintance with the rector and with the security of his aunt's coming to keep the rector's ladies at a distance, Verrell did not long delay calling at the rectory. He braved the hazards of the village street on foot defeating with a stony stare any who looked as though they hoped to speak to him. As he approached the rectory door he was brought to a stand by the glorious cascade of notes pouring from a window standing a little ajar. Someone was playing the second Allegro of Beethoven's 'Appassionata': but more than just playing . . . playing with power and rare talent. He stood entranced, unwilling to do anything to break the spinning web of sound thrown on the air. Twice the player checked and replayed a bar as though dissatisfied – but to the listener the performance was dazzling. Unless the Rothwells were entertaining an exceptionally talented visitor, the player, he decided, must be Mrs Rothwell. A lady of unexpected depths then to bring such a degree of understanding and feeling to the throbbing insistence of the piece. Only when the last quiet notes ended it did he enter the porch and sound the knocker.

'The rector's out, m'lord.' Jessie, young enough and unworldly enough to be in awe of speaking to a lord, brought her voice down from its first squeak, to add, 'So's the mistress. There's only Miss Daunton at home just now.'

He was relieved of the need to speak to the young lady since there was no one to chaperon her. Astonished and thoughtful, he left his card for the rector and walked away more slowly than he had come. The strains of the 'Moonlight Sonata' ghosted gently after him.

How could a girl not long out of the schoolroom produce the music he had heard? Even given a first-rate teacher, only an exceptional talent and dedicated application could produce such excellence in one so young.

That brought into his mind what his housekeeper had told him about Miss Daunton's visit to Herriards in the gloaming. Believing the new owner not yet in occupation, she had come, Mrs Penfold said, to take one more look at her old home and then had peered through the window hoping to see her piano. Mrs Penfold had found a pathos in that that he had refused to see. But now, whether he would or not, he was forced to consider the disruption in the girl's life caused by her father's bankruptcy and death. For the first time, it occurred to him that in a way, she was as much a victim of Anthony Daunton as he himself had been.

Even now he remembered the painful wrench with which he had left Mardens Hall, the anchor and frame of the first twenty-two years of his life. Lucy Daunton, at an even younger age, had been torn from her home as brutally and thrown on the world with fewer resources than he, as a man, had. And because she was her father's daughter, he had been blind to those facts.

Three weeks before Christmas, the rector told Lucy he had been asked to find a temporary companion for an elderly lady living two miles from Chalworth on the Tilchester road. A Mrs Montgomery. 'Have you any acquaintance with her?' he asked.

'I have heard her spoken of, but I do not know her.'

'She has a widowed daughter who lives with her and provides companionship, but an emergency in a younger, married sister's household has called her away. She is expected to be gone through Christmas and beyond. About six weeks in all. If you choose, I will recommend you for the post, but you must not think that we have any wish for you to go. We should much prefer to have you with us for the Christmas festival. On the other hand, it will give you an opportunity to discover if it is the kind of employment you really want. It is entirely your choice, my dear.'

To go to a strange house, among strangers, with Christmas approaching was not an attractive proposition, but, Lucy told herself sternly, it was something she might have to face more than once in the life that was now hers, so the sooner she accustomed herself to such changes the better. She signified her wish to go and it was arranged that the rector would drive her to Pixham House the following day and introduce her to Mrs Montgomery. If all went well, she could return to the rectory, pack up what she thought she would need and go back to Pixham House on whatever day was appointed.

The day was cold and grey, which did not help to relax Lucy's nerves on the journey to meet her first possible employer. It would be a different meeting from any she had ever experienced and she could only hope she would speak and do as she should.

Sensing something of this, Matthew Rothwell said encouragingly, 'Remember this meeting is for the purpose of discovering if you and Mrs Montgomery can be comfortable together. Even if the lady approves of you, but you feel you cannot be at ease with her, a look or a word to convey as much and I will intervene and we will come home.'

Pixham House was a plain and pleasant building standing in a small park. They were admitted by a very stately butler whom the rector addressed as Lawther, and were shown into a large and impressively furnished drawing-room where Mrs Montgomery awaited them.

Dressed in flowing black and purple garments against which her face and hands showed like pale wrinkled parchment stretched over strong bones, the lady possessed an imperious nose, a decided chin and a resolute mouth. She was old, but her pale eyes were bright and keenly enquiring.

The preliminary courtesies past, over Lucy's head, she said, 'So this is Anthony Daunton's daughter. She's on the small side, isn't she? Not frail, I hope?'

'No. Miss Daunton is perfectly healthy,' returned the rector austerely.

'Very young . . . very pretty.' Her tone suggested these attributes were to be deplored. For good measure she added, 'Beauty and brains don't always go together. I cannot abide fools.'

'You need have no fear on that score.' The rector's tone had become a little more tart.

Mrs Montgomery was undaunted. 'And reasonably educated, I take it?'

With difficulty, Lucy held her tongue and was startled a moment later to have a question shot at her. 'And you, miss . . .

do you consider yourself a sensible creature?'

'I think I have my share of common sense, ma'am,' Lucy answered as calmly as she could.

'Humph. Most girls your age don't have much. However, it seems there is paucity of choice and as close to Christmas as we are, I want the matter settled. So let us be done with it. You may come to me tomorrow. Mr Rothwell will give you a general idea of what is expected of you.'

'Is that acceptable to you, Lucy? the rector asked pointedly.

Though all her feelings were against it, Lucy nodded. 'Yes, sir.'

Brief as the meeting had been, it had been hard to endure and as they drove back to the rectory, Lucy sensed that the rector himself was not happy with it. Before long, he said, 'Mrs Montgomery showed herself in an unusually poor light today. She is an autocratic old lady who dislikes change and has been spoiled by her daughter. No doubt the idea of even temporary change has upset her. It is not too late for you to change your mind if you feel you cannot deal easily with her quirks.'

Lucy drew a deep breath. 'I should like to *try*, Mr Rothwell. I shall screw my courage to the sticking point and hope not to fail. Six weeks is not so very long." She gave him a small hopeful smile.

'Very well. If your mind is set on it. I shall visit Pixham House after a week or two and see how you are getting on. By that time, I shall hope to have someone in reserve who could take over from you if you are unhappy.'

CHAPTER NINE

Soon after ten the following morning, Lucy, back at Pixham House, was shown up to her room by a maid and informed that Mrs Montgomery was at present breakfasting in her room and would be descending the stairs about eleven o'clock.

Though at the back of the house and small, the room she had been allocated was reasonably comfortable. She unpacked and put away the clothes she had brought, then went downstairs and lingered in the hall until a servant appeared whom she could ask where she could wait until Mrs Montgomery came down.

'Best be the blue parlour, miss,' the man told her. ' 'Tis where the mistress sits most mornings.' He led her to the room and opened the door for her.

This room was on a much less grand scale than the drawing-room and to Lucy's eyes, was more attractive. The damask curtains were blue, as was the background colour of the garlanded carpet on which were set a number of chairs and a sofa covered in pale rose-shaded tabaret. A lively fire in the grate added a welcoming warmth and a well-filled bookcase drew her across the room. She was pleased to discover its contents covered a wide range, from contemporary novels and biographies to serious tomes dealing with such subjects as *The History of the*

Rebellion and Civil War in England, Civil Government and the ominously named *Letters from the Dead.*

She was looking through Boswell's *An Account of Corsica,* published a number of years ago, when the door opened and a sharp-toned voice said, 'So you are here!'

Lucy turned, gave a small curtsy and said, 'Good morning, ma'am.'

'Humph. We shall see,' Mrs Montgomery said unencouragingly and moved to seat herself in a chair by the fire. Pointing with her stick to a chair opposite, she said, 'Sit there.'

Lucy replaced the book she held on its shelf and did as she was bid. For long moments she was stared at in silence before the old lady spoke again. 'Well, young woman, I don't suppose you foresaw your future as what it is now. Your father brought things to a sorry pass, didn't he? A man of infinite charm, sadly given to doing what appeared expedient and lacking the sense to know when it will not serve. He lost his way after your mother died. She took the strength she lent him with her.'

Lucy remained silent.

'Nothing to say for yourself, miss?' Mrs Montgomery demanded.

Lucy's chin lifted fractionally. 'On the subject of my father, no, ma'am. I cannot discuss him with you or anyone.'

'Hoity-toity! In this house, *I* decide what subjects are discussed.'

'Of course, ma'am. But upon that subject I can only tell you I have nothing to say.'

The faded blue eyes glittered with annoyance, the stick beat a muffled tattoo on the carpeted floor, but after a time she said, 'A poor start. Very well, we shall not converse at all for the present. Instead, you may read to me. On the centre shelf of the bookcase you will find a book claimed by the author to have been written by a lady. Which is as may be. There is a marker at chapter twenty-one. Begin there.'

Lucy walked to the bookcase, turned and asked, 'The title, ma'am?'

Mrs Montgomery waved an impatient hand as though she had already given sufficient information. '*Emma. Emma*, of course.'

The book was lively and interesting and before long Lucy was hoping she could find opportunity to read the earlier chapters. It certainly made a pleasanter beginning to the day than what had been first offered.

Ten days passed before Matthew Rothwell came to Pixham House as promised. Lucy met him with a smile that took a little effort to produce. Mrs Montgomery had shown herself to be exacting, impatient and intolerant in ways that had chafed Lucy's spirit and made high demands on her good manners. There had been difficult moments and hours of boredom, but she had come through all without disaster and even managed to wring a small measure of respect from the old lady. She was able to tell the rector that she was willing to continue until Mrs Montgomery's daughter returned, though she could not bring herself to say she was happy to do so.

For her part, Mrs Montgomery grudgingly admitted that Miss Daunton had done no worse than she had expected and perhaps a little better than she had hoped.

The rector left reasonably satisfied and things continued to jog along fairly quietly as Lucy became more familiar with the old lady's likes, dislikes and customs.

Four days before Christmas, Lucy was in the dining-room arranging berries and ivy in a bowl for the table centrepiece. The fading light of a winter's afternoon meant lamps and candles were already being lit and curtains drawn. She took no notice of the sounds of a small bustle in the hall that reached her through the open door, but finished what she was doing and lifted the nearby candle to study her handiwork.

The man Lawther had just admitted to the house was now being conducted across the hall to the Blue Parlour, but he paused briefly as he passed the dining-room to look through the open doorway at the slim figure with upheld candle.

Satisfied at last with her arrangement, Lucy left the dining-room and was on her way to rejoin Mrs Montgomery when she heard a man's voice say, 'Who's the decorative little filly in the dining-room, Grandmama?'

She stopped short, heard the mutter of Mrs Montgomery's reply without being able to distinguish what was said then forced herself forward.

Entering the room, she saw the man who had spoken standing before the fire looking very much at home. Of average height, his strongly built figure was clothed fashionably but in country-style in a russet coat, mustard-coloured waistcoat and well-polished half-boots. He was, she thought, as she walked towards her employer, in his mid-twenties, with smooth skin over neat features that fell short of making him handsome.

Mrs Montgomery was looking pleased and said now, 'Come and meet my grandson, Miss Daunton. Believing me to be alone, he has come to cheer my Christmas, like the kind young man he is.'

His name was Fredrick Montgomery. Lucy had not liked his description of her, but she had not been meant to hear it and there was nothing in the way he responded to their introduction to which she could take exception. She sat down as Mrs Montgomery directed and so did her grandson as refreshments were carried in. The conversation that accompanied the Tokay and macaroons was almost entirely between grandmother and grandson, though Fredrick directed frequent smiling glances towards Lucy and now and then attempted to draw her into what was being discussed. He was she decided, kindly intentioned.

Three days later, her view of Fredrick Montgomery was very different.

The weather was now truly wintry with darkly grey days and a bitter wind. Heavy, sleety showers fell at intervals keeping all who had choice within doors. Card games and books were the chief amusements available at Pixham House and time passed slowly. If the weather had not been so relentlessly unpleasant, Fredrick might have spent some time riding about the countryside or visiting local acquaintance he had made on other visits to his grandmother. As it was, he endeavoured to add some spice to his days by setting up a flirtation with his grandmother's pretty temporary companion. Too often, Lucy found his hand on her arm or shoulder, even occasionally about her waist. Twice he trapped her in a passage and attempted to kiss her. When she told him she would be forced to complain to his grandmother if he persisted, he had laughed, saying, 'She wouldn't believe you, m'dear. Her little Freddie can do no wrong.' The confidence with which he spoke convinced her he spoke the truth.

On Christmas Eve, he began to drink quite early in the day and several times tried to induce Lucy to join him, quoting, '. . . 'tis the season to be merry.' When they went up to change for dinner that evening, Lucy found him following behind her as she went towards her room though his own was in the opposite direction among the larger bedchambers. Uneasy, she stopped and turning, attempted to go back past him, murmuring that she had left something downstairs.

He would not allow her to pass, but used his superior strength to pin her against the wall making her struggles ineffective.

'No escape this time, pretty maiden. Time to pay forfeit.' He held her helpless, his eyes glittering down at her in triumph. Then his mouth fastened on hers, moist, demanding and tasting of the brandy with which his breath was laden. It seemed to last forever before, needing air, he lifted his head.

She renewed her struggles but that only made him laugh. 'Silly little pigeon! Why don't you give in and have a bit of fun with me? Find out how nice I can be to a girl who's friendly?'

She read his intention to kiss her again and ducking her head, brought it up sharply under his chin. His mouth had been open and his lower jaw met the upper smartly with his tongue between. His hold on her loosened and she wrenched herself away. Reaching for her, his face contorted with rage and pain, he grabbed a handful of the bodice of her gown to pull her back to him. Being woollen the gown did not tear, but put under undue strain, several small buttons flew off and a stitch or two in the shoulder seam gave way. But she was free and taking to her heels, she ran. Hurling herself into her room, she slammed the door and turned the key in the lock.

The evening had little that was festive about it after that. Fredrick's enjoyment of the special dishes provided was spoiled by his sore tongue and Lucy, too apprehensive to eat much, jumped at the least sound. Mrs Montgomery was quickly aware of the unfavourable atmosphere and was irritated, but beyond rebuking her grandson for his lack of conversation, she delivered her chief reproofs to Lucy, accusing her of being in a sulk and inattentive.

The hours between the end of their six o'clock dinner and ten o'clock when Mrs Montgomery usually retired, had never dragged so slowly and Lucy had never been more relieved to hear her announce she wished to go to her bed. Gathering up the various articles Mrs Montgomery had scattered about the room throughout the day, among which was a *Book of Hours* that went everywhere with her but which she never opened, Lucy was ready to escort the old lady to her bedroom.

Fredrick went to bed at whatever time he chose, generally keeping the decanters company for an hour or two after his grandmother retired before doing so. Tonight, as Lucy passed close to him, without looking up he muttered, 'I'll have you yet, see if I don't.'

Following Mrs Montgomery upstairs, Lucy felt more than a little sick. When at last she was free to go to her own room, she scurried through the passages to reach her room and was thankful to reach it without encountering Fredrick. She turned the key in the lock again, relieved that both door and lock were sturdily made.

The small room was cosy. The heavy moreen curtains had been drawn across the window and muffled the sound of another shower of sleet hurling itself against the glass. A fire glowed warmly in the little basket-shaped grate and the candle standing on the night-table beside her bed had been lit. It was a virtue in Mrs Montgomery that she did not begrudge her companion such comforts. Adding a knob or two or sea-coal from the shining brass helmet nearby, Lucy sat beside the fire-glow, absorbing its agreeable warmth. How, she wondered, was she to get through tomorrow and the rest of Fredrick Montgomery's stay in the house? She saw no alternative to telling Mrs Montgomery of his assaults on her, but if she was not believed, what then?

It had been a long and wearing day and soon the warmth made her sleepy and she went to bed with her problem still unresolved.

Some small sound woke her in the black of the night. She did not know what it was and lay listening, waiting for it to be repeated. Then she heard it again . . . the faint squeak of the door handle being turned. The fire had fallen away to a feeble glimmer, too dull for sight to confirm what she heard. But now the lock was being shaken and was followed by a heavy thump on one of the door panels as though from an irritated fist.

All thought of sleep fled. For a long time she lay with all her attention concentrated on hearing any least sound that would tell her what was happening beyond her bedroom door. She heard nothing. Even the rain had ceased to assail the window. Leaving her bed, she began to dress. She had to get away, leave Pixham House. While Fredrick Montgomery was in it she was convinced she would not be safe.

Her clothes packed and a cloak over her dress, she pulled the curtain aside and peered out. The night pressed black and featureless against rain-blurred glass. She wondered what the time was and as though in answer to the thought, heard faint and far off the longcase clock in the hall strike five. Still two hours or more to dawn then and plenty of time to walk the two miles to Chalworth rectory. She could not carry the small trunk she had brought with her as well as the valise and she left it where it stood and went to the door. Her mouth dry with fear, she unlocked it and looked out, ready to slam the door shut again and turn the key. The passage beyond was as dark as the night outside.

Every nerve aquiver, afraid that Fredrick might yet be lurking somewhere waiting to pounce on her, she felt her way to the servants' stairs. Down these and on through other blind passages, she arrived at last at the side door for which she aimed. Only now did she begin to think she might escape successfully. She slid back the well-oiled top and bottom bolts without difficulty but then discovered there was no key. That, she realized, probably spent its nights in Lawther's charge. She would have to leave by a window. But which? The kitchens were semi-basement, its windows useless to her; the main rooms were raised several feet above ground level. She decided that one of the windows of the room with which she was most familiar was her best hope, and that meant the Blue Parlour. Unscrewing the bolt that secured the window she chose, she dropped the valise and then herself into the flowerbed beneath it to the detriment of the low shrubs on which she and her valise fell. These were leafy enough to transfer a generous share of the icy rainwater they bore to her clothes and, as she straightened up, mud squelched over the top of her shoes. It was an uncomfortable start but she was safely out of the house.

The night was still as impenetrably black as it had appeared from the bedroom window and she located the path that would lead her to the main carriageway as much by luck as judgement. Once there, the scrunch of gravel under her feet was her best guide to the gates, though she blundered more than once on to verges and only some sixth sense saved her from colliding with the iron gates when they reared up before her.

She felt her way to the Judas-gate and went through it into the lane. As she turned towards Chalworth, the first drops of another heavy shower began to fall.

The unrelenting darkness forced her to walk slowly, but telling herself that two miles was no great distance, she went forward resolutely. She soon found that stinging sleet and the fiercely gusting wind that blew under her cloak and whirled its hood off her head, made formidable extra difficulties. By the time she had trudged half a mile, she was drenched to the skin, cold through to her bones and plastered with mud from a fall. Both her cloak and her valise had become sodden weights and at the end of the first mile she was close to tears of exhaustion.

Somehow she forced herself to plod on, but when the next savage onslaught of sleet began she knew she could go no further without respite. Her mind was beginning to play tricks. Twice her valise had slipped from her icy fingers and she felt herself wanting to sink to the ground and cower there, letting the elements do their worst. Vaguely she was aware there were trees on the right-hand side of the lane and though in their leafless state they could offer little shelter, they might give some protection from the driving wind and sleet.

There was a ditch between lane and trees and memory offered no help towards judging how deep it was. She went into it in a sliding fall. It was deep and the bottom held about a foot of water. She made several attempts to heave herself out on the far side but the muddy ground offered no purchase for her feet and she could reach nothing by which she might have hauled herself out. In the end her exhausted body refused further co-operation and she slid back to the bottom of the ditch beyond helping herself.

CHAPTER TEN

To be roughly shaken awake by Penfold's hand on his shoulder was sufficiently unusual to bring Verrell to his full senses at once. As he reared up, Penfold leapt back from the bed, the candle he carried tilting dangerously.

' 'Tis gypsies, sir. Two of 'em. Must see " 'im of the house" is all they'll say,' he said in breathless explanation.

'At this hour! What time *is* it, for heaven's sake?'

'Dawn. Or thereabouts.'

'And Christmas Day! Tell them I'll see them tomorrow at a reasonable hour.'

'One's carrying a young woman. The one that lived here . . . came here once. In a bad way. Covered in mud. Dead. Swooned. I dunno.'

'In God's name, man! Why did you not say that first! Pass me my robe.' Verrell thrust his legs out of bed, his feet into slippers and his arms into the robe Penfold held out. Taking the candle from the man, he was halfway to the door as he demanded, 'Where are they?'

'Kitchen door.' Then, remembering, threw after him as he disappeared, 'Sir.'

Opening the door on the outside world that Penfold had cautiously closed and bolted against the early callers, Verrell saw beyond it a man, a boy of about twelve and two skewbald ponies. They waited motionless as carvings under a paling sky crossed by wind-driven lumbering cloud. The boy had dismounted and stood a little in advance, his saddleless pony's reins in one hand and a soaked and muddy valise in the other. The man's pony was saddled and its headstall was of silver-studded scarlet leather. He sat his shaggy steed like a king on a caparisoned charger despite the bedraggled bundle he held before him: a handsome man, dark-skinned, hawk-nosed and black of eye and hair. His own age or a year or so younger, Verrell judged, as he stepped on to the damp flags, and enough likeness between him and the boy for them to be father and son. Both regarded him with looks of royal detachment.

For a full minute the three remained in silent appraisal before the man asked, 'Him of the house?'

'Verrell. Yes.' His gaze now on the man's inanimate burden, Verrell asked, 'Is she dead?'

A minute shake of the head answered him.

'Where? How?'

'A ditch. The edge of Merles' Wood. Your wood.' Your wood, your responsibility, his tone said without waste of words.

'You passed the rectory to come here. Why did you not take her there?'

The question produced not the least flicker of understanding in the man's face and Verrell guessed he did not know Miss Daunton now lived there. He said, 'Give her to me,' and walking past the boy, held up his arms.

The man made no movement. 'Has she a welcome?'

'Great heavens, yes! I would not turn a dog from the house in the state she appears to be in.'

Still the man did not move, but let his black gaze remain locked to Verrell's as though assessing the value of his words. Several moments passed before he stirred, shifted his hold on the girl and bent to pass her to him.

In the moment in which Verrell looked down at Lucy Daunton's white, unconscious face, the boy dropped the valise on to the path, swung on to his pony and the pair wheeled about and was gone.

As he turned back into the house, the girl's sodden garments were already making their dampness felt through the sleeves of his heavy brocade robe.

To Penfold, hovering uncertainly in the kitchen, he said, 'Ask Mrs Penfold to come to me in the smaller drawing-room as soon as possible, then bring in the valise you'll find outside.' He walked through to the room he had named to lay his mud-plastered burden down on a sofa heedless of its pale silk covering.

Mrs Penfold hurried into the room as he straightened. 'Poor young thing!' she exclaimed looking down at Lucy. She set down the lamp she carried 'Whatever has happened to her, sir?'

'I don't know, but I intend to find out. Get her stripped and warmed and do what you can to bring her back to consciousness. I'll send someone for the doctor and go to the rectory myself.'

'It's Ashwick for Dr Walsh and Christmas Day, too,' the house-keeper reminded him.

'I'll send a note and a carriage,' he said, in a tone that expressed his unreadiness to accept any possibility of the doctor failing to attend. 'Is Mrs Gresham awake?'

'I've no knowing, sir. It's early yet. I planned to take up her chocolate about eight of the clock, which she is what she asked for.'

'Tell her, with my apologies, that I have need of her here right away and not to waste time dressing.' It occurred to him that, having come to Herriards only the previous day, Julia's stay was to have an odd start.

Less than half-an-hour later, note and carriage despatched to the doctor and himself washed, shaved and dressed, he re-entered the room where Lucy Daunton lay to find the sofa had been pushed close to the fireplace where a fire was doing its best to produce heat. The sofa was now layered with blankets and the girl's small figure half lost in them. Julia Gresham, in a dressing-gown and with her greying hair in a plait, knelt beside the sofa, trying to coax a few more drops of brandy down the girl's throat. She looked up at him.

'Now and then she opens her eyes, but she's not really conscious. She is utterly exhausted, I think.'

'Is she warm?'

'She's warming. The kitchen girl's bringing a hot brick for her feet and Mrs Penfold's making chocolate for her. Who is she? Do you know?'

'Miss Daunton. Lucy Daunton.'

'*Daunton!*' The name struck home at once. 'Related to—'

'His daughter.'

'Where does she live?'

'Here in Chalworth. The rector gave her a home when her own was sold up.'

'And that was here? In this village?'

'It was this house.'

She gave him a startled, frowning look. 'You did not tell me that.'

'There has hardly been occasion to do so. I was not expecting this.' He spoke indifferently and turned to the door before Julia could say more. 'I am going to the rectory now. I should not be long.' As he went out into the hall, he passed Mrs Penfold carry-ing the chocolate and behind her, a young, tousle-haired maid with a flannel-wrapped brick.

He walked with impatient speed through the chill dampness of the morning to the rectory and asked to see the rector on a matter of some urgency. As usual with such requests, he was shown into the rector's study. He did not sit down but stood at the window staring out at the winter-sad garden, turning when Matthew Rothwell entered.

'Lord Verrell . . .' Matthew's tone was surprised, enquiring. 'What can I do for you? Do please be seated.' He indicated a chair and moved round his desk.

Verrell remained standing. 'At dawn this morning two gypsies, a man and a boy, brought Miss Daunton to my house. They had found her in a ditch, less than half a mile outside Chalworth. She was unconscious, coated with mud and soaked to the skin. She had a valise with her.'

Shocked, Matthew said nothing. Verrell's stark recital matched the cold grey stare of his lordship's eyes. No man, Matthew thought, had ever looked at him more coldly. Meeting the challenge banked behind that bleak regard, he asked quietly, 'And. . . ?'

'Was she coming to or going from here?'

'Most certainly coming to it.'

Only then did Verrell relax and sit down. 'I beg your pardon, Rector. I thought it would be so, but I needed to be certain. But where had she been? Why was she out on such a night? On *any* night. And on foot!'

'Why she was out I don't know. But I shall certainly make it my business to find out.'

'But where had she been?'

Matthew told him, adding, 'It is not our wish, but she insists she must find a way to support herself. I visited Lucy a week ago and all seemed well. If not quite happy, she was proud to be managing and even winning a certain amount of goodwill from the old lady. Mrs Montgomery is an overbearing woman, but I know no worse of her. I cannot think what has happened. What has Lucy said?'

'Nothing sensible so far. She has not been fully conscious yet. I have sent to Ashwick for Dr Walsh. He should be on his way by now. Meanwhile my aunt, Mrs Gresham, and my housekeeper are caring for her.'

'My wife will want her back in her own charge as soon as she hears what has happened. We have made ourselves responsible for Lucy and have grown fond of her. I am, however, committed to taking the morning service at ten. An important one in the Church calendar, you will understand.'

'Yes, of course. If the doctor allows, I will bring Miss Daunton to you after that.'

'But you yourself are unlikely to appear in church?'

Verrell gave him a slanting smile and said obliquely, 'Mrs Gresham may wish to attend.'

Matthew's answering smile was equally enigmatic. 'The pew reserved for Herriards will always be available.'

They parted then. Matthew saw him to the door and stood in thought for several minutes after Verrell had disappeared from sight. It was obvious Verrell had done all that could be done for Lucy. He had also taken the trouble to be sure she was not in flight *from* the rectory. But his manner throughout had been detached, and he had expressed no sympathetic concern for the girl. '*And though I give my body to be burned and have not charity—*' Inevitably the words came into his mind. Was it that Verrell, though a responsible man, was not warm-hearted? Or was it that he could find no warmth for Anthony Daunton's daughter? Verrell was a complex man and certainly not one to be easily read. He wondered how well Verrell read himself.

100

THE CHOICE

*

Lucy passed out of the gate of dreams to find herself warm in her bed at the rectory and no recollection of how she had arrived there. Brief snatches of memory came to her of a nightmare of fear and desperation that had begun at Pixham House; of stinging hail, freezing wind and unrelieved darkness. It had been the strengthening grip of icy coldness that had finally robbed her of strength to continue her fight against the weather and mud that clutched at her feet as though never to let go. How it had all ended, she had no recall, though vague impressions floated through her mind of having been carried on a horse, lain on a sofa at Herriards, been tended by a woman she had never seen before. She thought, too, she had heard Lord Verrell's voice once or twice, but nothing was fixed or certain.

Hearing some slight sound now, she opened her eyes and, turning her head, saw Susan sitting beside her, a book in her lap but her gaze fixed on distance. Her small movement brought Susan's gaze to her at once. 'You're awake! You really are, aren't you? Oh, Lucy it's been so long!' She bent to kiss Lucy's cheek. 'I must go and tell Mama. We have all been so worried.'

Her voice a soft croak, Lucy said, 'Wait . . . please wait. Tell me . . . how did I get here?'

'Lord Verrell brought you. In his carriage, with Mrs Gresham, an aunt who is staying with him at present.'

'Lord Verrell! But from where did he bring me?'

'Two gypsies found you unconscious in a ditch at dawn this morning. Not knowing, I suppose, that you live here now, they took you to Herriards.' She rose from her chair. 'But Mama will tell you the rest. I promised I would let her know the instant you woke, so I must go to her now.'

101

Matthew Rothwell came with his wife to see Lucy and heard a brief, halting outline of the reasons for her flight from Pixham House. His attentive gaze fixed on her face, he listened to her, himself saying nothing. When her tale was done, he simply patted her hand where it lay on the coverlet and left the room.

'I'm sorry . . . sorry to be so troublesome. But I could not stay there. He wanted— He would have— And now I'm spoiling your Christmas Day!' Her whispering voice died as tears brimmed.

'Nothing of the sort,' said Mrs Rothwell robustly. 'Of course you could not stay there! And we knew nothing about it until Lord Verrell came to see the rector and told him where you were.'

'It was probably Hyram Smith who took me to Herriards. Hyram has been head of the family since his father, Aaron, died. He and his mother together.'

'If it was so, we all have reason to be grateful to him. Lord Verrell and Mrs Gresham, the aunt who has come to live with him, brought you here after morning service. They had done all that could be done for you. Doctor Walsh had seen you and pronounced that you had passed from coma into deep sleep and providing there were no ill results from the cold and the soaking you suffered, you have nothing to fear. He will call here tomorrow to see how you go on.'

'But your day – Christmas Day – has been quite cut up through me!'

'Not at all. It is not yet two o'clock. So you see there are still plenty of hours left in the day and you have no need to concern yourself. As soon as the rector returns from Pixham House, we shall have our Christmas dinner very little later than we planned.'

'But Mr Rothwell has had to go to Pixham House!'

'My dear Lucy, you should know by now that he is no stranger to being called out at any time of the day or night, Christmas Day or not. Don't be gooseish. What has surprised him is that Mrs Montgomery should have sent no message regarding your sudden departure.' She smiled reassuringly at the girl. 'We are truly glad to have you back with us. Rest now, and if you feel able you shall come down to dinner in your dressing-gown and stay as long as is comfortable for you. But if you have not the strength for it, you shall have your meal in bed.'

Left alone, Lucy wondered what Lord Verrell would have done if his aunt had not been with him when she had been taken to Herriards. Would he have told them to carry their unwanted burden to the rectory where it belonged? She could not believe that he would have willingly accepted her as having a claim on his humanity if he could have passed the responsibility to someone else. She could almost see the look of contempt on his face when he saw her as she must have looked then.

Christmas dinner at Herriards was served at five o'clock. Verrell and Julia, mellowed by good food and good wine, lingered over nuts and sweetmeats, talking of other times, other Christmases, and from those went on to speak of what he had done in India and Burma and of his occasional visits to Europe that never extended to England.

He had just ended one of his reminiscences when Julia said musingly, 'There is a touch of severity in the way you view things, Harry, that brings your father to mind. I remember my sister telling me that at times she had to beg him not to be too exacting where you children were concerned.'

Verrell laughed. 'You're a long way out if you think me a strict moralist. I could tell you tales of some of my dealings with rival merchants that would make you blush for me.'

'Oh, when a man's pulling the devil by the tail he can be forgiven much. But now and then I hear echoes of my brother-in-law in what you say and perhaps rather more in what you don't say. Anthony Daunton failed you as a friend and your father failed you by doubting your innocence. . . . Louise told me how bitter you were when you first returned to England . . . are you still so?'

'Would you not be so, Julia? Daunton and my father – each in his way betrayed me. My father's betrayal was the worse, though that too, could be laid to Daunton's charge.'

'Many said Daunton was a broken reed after his wife's death. You did not deserve what happened to you, Harry, I know. But don't tell me you are sorry for yourself.'

'Sorry, no. But there is a lingering anger in me I seem unable to subdue. What I am sorry for is the loss of the man I might have been . . . was bred to be. I am not the one who was in the making. Stronger, perhaps. Better? I think not.'

'You were always a kind young man. Are you not so now?'

'One of the first lessons I learned after leaving these shores was that many men regard kindness as a weakness. So kindness and I had to part company. Another thing I learned was the importance of winning. At all times, in all circumstances.'

His bleak look touched her, moved her to say, 'It is only four months since you returned to live in this country. Barely three since you came to live in Chalworth. Give yourself time and you may find you have not changed so very much.'

'A hopeful philosophy, Julia. You would be unwise to build on it where I am concerned though.'

There was a brief silence before Julia said, 'Tell me the worst that happened to you. The worst thing you did?'

'I have already told you the worst that happened. Painful as it was to lose my home, my identity, my country and to suffer the hardships of the early years, none of it compared with my father refusing to believe what I told him. *That* I cannot forgive. Shall *never* forgive!'

'Your father, Harry! Remember the good years.'

'It is not my father I cannot forgive. It is Daunton. But the thing that sticks in my craw as the worst thing I ever did, involves my father. No more than a petty crime in the circumstances, I suppose, and yet—' He shook his head and left the sentence unfinished. 'When I decided I must get out of the country, Julia, I forced the central drawer in Father's desk and stole a hundred sovereigns. I say I stole, but I left him an IOU which I had every intention of honouring.' He laughed on a short, jarring note. 'Something else his death precluded. Something else I cannot forgive Daunton.'

Julia gazed thoughtfully into the wine that remained in the glass cradled in her hands. When, presently, she looked up, she asked, 'And how do you view little Miss Daunton?'

Harry frowned, shrugged, said, 'In no particular way. I did not know when I came to Chalworth that she was still living here. I bought the house because I knew something of it and liked it better than others I was offered at the time.'

'In a small village like this you must have encountered her occasionally. As her father's daughter, you cannot regard her exactly as you would do any other young woman. It is to be expected that I shall meet her too and I need to know what your feelings are towards her.'

His meetings with Miss Daunton came all too readily to mind, the first the most memorable. His disclaimer had not been quite honest, though he could not say with any certainty how he viewed Miss Daunton. What was certain was that thought of her muddled his feelings into a mixture of frustration and irritation. Looking across the table at his aunt, he said with a hint of exasperation, 'I will tell you the tale of my first encounters with the young lady and you may judge for yourself.'

He began with his unexpected introduction to the Rothwells

and Miss Daunton at the Assembly Rooms' ball and his friend, Peter Eddis, subsequently taking him gently to task for failing to dance with the girl.

'Peter also wondered why I had chosen to buy Herriards and come here to live. I chose to tell him as unpleasantly as I could that it must be to seduce, rape or murder Miss Daunton. I was a guest in his house at the time, yet I did not hold back from insulting him further before coming to my senses and apologizing. Peter, being the good fellow he is, with far more grace than I shall ever attain, forgave me my crass discourtesy.'

Julia looked at him with understanding sympathy and said softly, 'Poor Harry!'

'Poor *Harry*! Don't waste your sympathy,' he said harshly. 'I had not run my length. Feeling in need of a period of solitude, I made my way to one of the small rooms at the back of the building. The one I entered was lit only by firelight. A moment too late, I discovered it was not untenanted as I had thought it. When I could pierce its shadows, I found I was sharing it with the root cause of my discomfort . . . Miss Daunton. If only it had not been *her*! I suppose because she was Anthony's daughter, I at once assumed the worst . . . supposed her there to keep an assignation with the young man who had supplied her with a partner when I failed her. Needing further outlet for my ill temper, I took it on myself to lecture her on her impropriety. When she, quite properly, told me that what she did was no concern of mine, I abandoned words and gave her practical demonstration of the dangers she was supposedly inviting.'

Julia looked dismayed. 'What *did* you do?'

'I kissed her. In no loverlike way. With brutal unkindness.'

Julia sighed. 'And then. . . ?'

'And then,' Verrell said, 'in the moment in which I took in the depths of her shock and innocence, the door opened and the person for whom she had been waiting came in. Another young girl who stood and stared almost as shocked as Miss Daunton.'

'How did it end?'

He snorted a cynical laugh. 'As it should, you might say. In my complete rout. God knows who was her model, but the chit drew herself up to her full small height and directed her friend to leave the door open because the gentleman was going. And she gave the word *gentleman* all the scepticism it deserved. Perhaps that should rank alongside the hundred sovereigns I stole. Something done against a young girl – little more than a child – and not done under the stress of necessity, but through peevish ill-temper.'

Attempting to lighten his unhappy mood, Julia said lightly, 'Don't give either act too much importance. In Miss Daunton's case, you were unhorsed by a schoolgirl and, as you say, deserved to be. Are you now ostracized by the village?'

'No. Oddly, neither Miss Daunton nor her friend appears to have passed the story on. Why, I do not know. But I have been glad to be sheltered by their reticence from the condemnation I deserve.'

'Does the rector not know?'

'No. And for that I am very much in Lucy Daunton's debt because he is a man who engaged my respect from our first meeting. I should be sorry to lose his.'

'Have you met the girl since? She must be terrified of you.'

'When we meet her eyes betray she expects no good of me. But young as she is, Miss Daunton has more backbone than her father. Like David facing Goliath with nothing more than his slingshot, she stands her ground.'

Julia was tempted to say, *And look what happened to Goliath*, but was diverted by the thought that Verrell's problem might well be that he was two men in one . . . the 'might have been' and what the years of exile had made of him. It was time, she thought, to change the subject, and did so.

CHAPTER ELEVEN

Mrs Gresham and Lord Verrell called at the rectory the following day to enquire how Lucy was progressing. They were told that Dr Walsh had seen her again that morning and had said that as no cold or chill appeared to be developing from her exposure, she was doing well and a day or two resting in bed should see her quite recovered.

Mrs Gresham asked if she might be allowed to see the young lady and was shown up to her bedroom.

Lucy recognized the slim, intelligent-looking woman whom Mrs Rothwell brought to be introduced as the one who, in her rather hazy recollections, had held brandy to her lips and coaxed her to swallow. She liked what she saw now: the grey-blue eyes were shrewd, but there was something in Mrs Gresham's face that hinted at a readiness to be amused. Realizing that some of the dreamlike impressions she had were gathered from intermittent returns to consciousness, she attempted to express her thanks for the lady's attentions.

These were smilingly brushed aside. 'No, no. I am not here to be thanked but to see that you are on the road to recovery and, happily, it appears that you are. I am likely to be in Chalworth for some time and I hope when you are quite restored you will come to see me.'

Her visit was brief but when she and Mrs Rothwell left her, Lucy did not feel that its brevity came from anything other than a desire not to tire her.

Discussing their visitors when they had gone, Mrs .Rothwell and Susan agreed that Mrs Gresham would make a pleasant and friendly addition to Chalworth society and cautiously acknowledged that Lord Verrell improved on closer acquaintance.

'Though all the enquiries about Lucy came from Mrs Gresham,' Susan pointed out. 'Lord Verrell hardly mentioned her.'

'But he did everything that was necessary when she had need of help.'

Susan was sceptical. 'It might have been only at Mrs Gresham's prompting.'

'Let us be generous and assume honours are to be shared equally between them,' Mrs Rothwell said, ending the discussion.

Mid-way through the first dour and chilly week of January, Verrell and Mrs Gresham sat at after-dinner ease in front of a handsome fire in the smaller drawing-room. Looking up from the list of names she had written on the tablet on her knee, Julia said, 'Harry, you have lived here for three months . . . have you met none but the rectory people? What have you been doing? Acting the recluse?'

'There has been a great deal to occupy my attention. I have not needed, or wanted, distraction.'

She gave him a quizzing look and said mockingly, 'Is distraction the best you think your neighbours can provide? And now you want to give a dinner-party but have no acquaintance on whom to draw except the three Rothwells and their protégée and *she*, you say, may choose not to come. Is everyone else in the village beneath your notice?'

Verrell looked startled. 'No, of course not! Heavens, Julia, what have I to be top-lofty about?'

'A title is often enough. And that is how your neighbours may look upon your being so inaccessible. However, we will make shift to remedy the matter. So tell me, who are the great and interesting ones of the village?'

He gave her a twisted smile. 'After me, you mean? The Hammonds occupy the only other considerable house, but they are away. In London I believe, for reasons to do with Mrs Hammond's health. I have that from Naylor, the groom I brought over from Mardens Hall. Do you remember him? He insists on giving me local news whether I wish for it or not. Whom else to invite, I simply do not know. We could discover if Peter Eddis is home again and less encumbered by family affairs than he has been. He lives in Ashwick, so is not too far away. Doctor Walsh too. Having met him three or four times in his professional capacity I suppose I may claim acquaintance.'

'It seems to me I shall do better consulting Naylor,' said his aunt a trifle acidly.

'Oh, by far. And there are always the halt and the lame if all else fails.'

'Can you point out even those?' Julia shook her head in frustration. 'Another thing, you need more staff. A cook foremost. Mrs Penfold has enough to do as housekeeper. A butler, too, if you are to live as you should. Penfold is not comfortable in the role. Let him be designated upper servant, which will give him equal status and keep him happy. A footman would be useful and at the very least two chambermaids to supplement the kitchen maid and the two women who come in. Can you afford so much?'

'Easily, and more if you see the need. Hire whom you choose and as many as you choose. I shall be more than happy to leave all that in your hands.'

'And be excused from any effort on your part, my lord?'

'Just so. Except where the stables are concerned. Am I taxing you beyond your abilities, dear Aunt?'

She looked at him with sparks in her eyes. 'Let me tell you, young Harry—'

'Ah, that's much better!' He leaned across to take up one of her hands and kiss it lightly. '*My lord* had me worried that you were on the point of packing your bags and washing your hands of me.'

'Not while there is a spark of humour left in you to give me hope that the Sisyphean labour of hauling you back into the human race is worth while.'

Though jokingly said, her intention was serious. And since he had taken a step in the right direction by proposing a dinner-party, she must do her best to assemble a sufficient and harmonious company of guests. His motive, she supposed, was to further his friendship with the rector whom he had made plain he both liked and respected. And Harry, she had discovered, respected very few people these days.

The Rothwells were quietly pleased with the invitation to dine at Herriards that arrived a week later. Told that the invitation included her, Lucy would have been happy to excuse herself from going. She was not sure that she could enter Herriards as a guest and see without discomfort the changes that were sure to have been made in the house. Still more painful would be seeing the man her father had injured paramount in his place: whatever Anthony Daunton had done or not done, he was her father. She had loved him and still did.

Mrs Rothwell regarded her understandingly when she voiced her doubts. 'It is bound to be difficult for you, my dear, I do see. But might it not appear ungracious if you do not go when you have so recently had reason to be much obliged to both Lord Verrell and Mrs Gresham? The first occasion will be the worst. If others follow, they can never be so bad again.'

Lucy could not do other than bow to her reasoning. What she could not reveal to the rector's wife were certain memories relating to Lord Verrell that induced feelings far different from that of obligation.

The rectory party was greeted generally and with pleasant warmth by their host and hostess. Lucy kept as much in the background as she could and was careful not to allow her gaze to meet Lord Verrell's.

Mrs Gresham had prayed that the guests she had managed to assemble would prove a harmonious group. She was soon assured of some success. Though not yet able to come to Herriards for the promised visit, Sir Peter Eddis was here tonight with his sister, Mrs Lingard, and her husband. Happening to catch the look exchanged between Sir Peter and Susan Rothwell on first seeing each other, it was evident to Mrs Gresham that she had two guests more than pleased with their company.

Doctor Walsh had proved to be a widower but he had a daughter of twenty-three still living at home who was engaged to a naval officer at present abroad on a tour of duty. Eleven people sat down to the elegant meal Mrs Gresham and the new cook had devised between them. It was an awkward number to seat but the oval table in the smaller of Herriards' two dining-rooms made the best of what could be done with it.

For all the good intentions she had made, Lucy could not prevent her jealous gaze from seeking out change in the house she loved so well. She found few had been made and most of those in the room they were now in. Here there was a handsome new carpet on the floor and fine silver she had not seen before on both sideboard and table. The beautiful crystal glasses in which wine was served were also strange to her and were engraved with a crest she supposed was Lord Verrell's. None of these changes could be said to have been made for change's sake. Her attention was drawn away from her inventory by Doctor Walsh who was her right-hand neighbour and thereafter she was given little time for further introspection.

Some time later, replete and relaxed, everyone sat in the larger drawing-room comfortably warmed by generous fires at each end of its length. When conversation flagged for a moment, Lord Verrell stepped in to suggest that the younger ladies might be willing to entertain the company with a little music. Lucy had already noticed that the single change in this room was that the piano that had once been hers had been brought into it.

Mrs Rothwell immediately put forward Miss Walsh's name, claiming that she played delightfully. Without affecting unnecessary modesty, Miss Walsh obliged with two cheerful cavatinas, and remained at the piano afterwards to accompany Susan when the doctor mentioned that Susan had a very pretty voice and she was invited to sing.

Beginning a little nervously, very conscious of a particular presence, Susan sang two of Burns's lyrics, 'John Anderson, my Jo' and 'A Red, Red Rose' in a sweet, untrained voice that gathered strength as she sang and visibly touched her audience.

Since the Rothwells had heard only the simpler pieces of her repertoire, Lucy hoped she could meet any invitation to play in such a way as to hint at inadequacy without actually lying. The escape was not allowed her. When Susan and Miss Walsh returned to their seats, Lord Verrell said with a certainty that astonished her, 'And now Miss Daunton.' Walking to the piano, he selected a sheaf of music from among the rest on its top and stood waiting expectantly for her.

Lucy could not do other than follow the example set for her by the other two girls and comply without fuss. Reluctantly she went to take the seat at the instrument resolved to play only a barcarolle and, if she must, follow it with a rondoletto, both conveniently short. She was defeated in this too.

'You will favour us with Beethoven's 'Apassionata', will you not?' Lord Verrell said with a curious smile, setting the music he held on the easel.

Lucy looked her astonishment. 'That is no easy piece, my lord.'

'I am aware.'

'Why should you suppose I am able?'

'Do you say you are not?'

She turned away from the glinting challenge in his eyes and looking down at the keyboard, murmured, 'I am not in practice.'

'Sufficiently so to give us all great pleasure, I am sure,' was the suave rejoinder.

'The piece is too long.' She made a last desperate protest.

'Then play only the third movement, the second Allegro.'

There was to be no escape, she saw. He had the music open and ready at the right page. Hardly knowing that she did so, she let her fingers drift lovingly, soundlessly, over the familiar keyboard before playing the quiet opening notes and the double motif that followed. As her fingers flowed into the first of the long brilliant downrun of notes she forgot Lord Verrell's daunting nearness, forgot the other listeners and entered the special world that music opened to her.

There was something startled in the silence that held her listeners at the end, a silence the doctor broke with a sudden, explosive, 'God bless my soul!' which released the others to applaud.

'Bravo, Miss Daunton,' Lord Verrell said quietly. 'Not only a pianist but a musician . . . power and passion never out of control.' He paused, before adding still more quietly, 'Even when angry, as you were when I first asked you to play.' He held out a hand to her, smiling in a way that told her he knew just how much she had resented being coerced into playing the piece he had chosen. 'Anything more just now would be anti-climax, I think, so you are excused,' he finished.

The hand she laid in his quivered with the force of her feelings.

She was expecting to be conducted back to her seat beside Susan, but before it was reached, Mrs Gresham said, 'Bring Miss Daunton to me, if you please, Harry,' and she was led to a chair beside her hostess.

'Not to beat about the bush, Miss Daunton, such talent as you have should not be hid.' Mrs Gresham's blue-grey eyes were bright with interest. 'Tell me, who is your teacher?'

'I no longer have one, ma'am. I was used to be taught by Professor Lowson who has an academy of music in Tilchester.'

'Indeed! I have heard of him. But to have broken off your studies is little short of crim—' She broke off, looking vexed. 'I beg your pardon. How very thoughtless of me. Do forgive me. It is just that your playing is so exceptional. Especially for one so young. Believe me, for in my time, I have heard the best there is.'

'Later, when their guests had gone, and she and Verrell were drinking a nightcap beside one of the dying fires, Julia said, 'You knew that young girl could produce a virtuoso performance, didn't you, Harry? She went to the piano reluctantly and you stood there with the Beethoven music in your hand and argued her into playing what you had selected. Furthermore, I would

116

swear you were the only one in the room who knew what to expect. So how did you?'

He gave her a gleaming look. 'Chance, Julia. Nothing more. I called at the rectory one day when everyone but Miss Daunton was out and I overheard her playing the piece. I was outside on the garden path. She did not know.'

'And despite twelve years in the wilderness you recognized the quality of what you heard!'

'I was not bred up a philistine, my dear, as you know. And in the later years of my exile, my occasional visits to Vienna and other civilized capitals that were not currently in Napoleon's hands were as much for my soul's refreshment as for business.'

'Did you not sense as I did that no one else in the room knew how well she played? I thought it odd that the Rothwells did not appear to know. The poor child must be very unhappy that she can no longer study with Professor Lowson and tonight you may have made her more unhappy by forcing her to reveal what she had chosen to keep hidden.'

'I did not know it was so and do not pretend to understand it. If I *had* known, I think I should still have invited her to play.'

She gave him a shrewd, considering look. 'To what end, Harry?'

'Having heard her, what other answer do you need?'

'To know if there is one.'

Harry smiled and shook his head. But not, she thought, in absolute denial.

To Lucy's relief neither the rector nor his wife remarked upon her playing. Only Susan, before they got into bed that night, said, 'Lucy, I feel such a pig about the piano, but I had no idea you play as you do.' Looking a little shame-faced, she explained about her one-time wish to be offered a seat in the Herriards carriage. 'I was a ninny, I know, to expect you to guess what I wanted, but I was only fifteen and you know how it is then. You *will* use the piano now, won't you? To show that you really forgive me.'

Lucy agreed. But she was uncertain of how she felt at having her talent dragged into view. How had Lord Verrell known about it? And then, unable to suppress the familiar initial stab of apprehension, she wondered *why* he had done it.

CHAPTER TWELVE

February had only just given way to March when Matthew Rothwell stood regarding the two girls standing a little nervously on the other side of his desk. That what he was about to tell them would please them, he was sure: what he himself disliked about it was what he was committed to *not* telling Lucy. The omission implied an untruth made all the more uncomfortable by giving him credit where none was due. It was only for Lucy's sake he had agreed to it and his hope was that he would not be called on actually to lie to her.

With carefully assumed lightness, he said, 'I take it both you talented young ladies are prepared for hard work?'

'Talented?' Susan was instantly suspicious. 'Papa, what do you mean?'

'As I think you know, Lord Verrell came to see me a little over a week ago. Some part of our conversation turned to your musical performances on the evening of Mrs Gresham's dinner-party. As a consequence, learning that there was a difficulty regarding regular transport to take you to Tilchester to study your diverse arts, he was kind enough to offer to put a light chaise and a reliable driver at your joint disposal. Since then I have seen both Señor Contarini and Professor Lowson and arranged that your courses of instruction will begin this coming Wednesday at ten in the morning in each case.'

'Oh Papa!' Susan was ecstatic. 'Is it really so? I can hardly believe it!'

'I suggest you put it to the test by being shawled and bonneted in good time next Wednesday.' He held up a hand as Susan drew breath to launch into speech again. 'Save anything more you have to say for each other's ears and reward me now with a quiet study to prepare to deal with the parish clerk's latest alarms. You will, of course, wish to write letters of appreciation to Lord Verrell.'

Susan darted round the desk to plant a rapturous kiss on her father's cheek before dancing from the room, but Lucy lingered. Lord Verrell's provision of transport she saw as a compliment to the rector and her inclusion as incidental and therefore accept- able. The concern she felt was for something else and she said, 'Sir, there is the matter of Professor Lowson's fees . . . .'

'Do not trouble your head over those, my dear.'

'But I must. Living here, I am every day in your debt and I am all too aware that I have no real claim on your generosity. It cannot be right for me to take even more from you, especially for something that is not essential.'

'If we are to speak of debts, Lucy, I must tell you that with no more right than you claim to have on me, I had the living of St Cyriac's from your father's hands, which was a greater gift than I could possibly have hoped for from any direction at the time. So you see in the matter of obligation there is more on my side than on yours. If we are of use to each other, that is as it should be. And you will be of use to Susan, as she will be to you, in chap- eroning one another on your journeys to and from Tilchester. So say no more about it.'

His tone was too firm for her to continue to protest and though

120

still uneasy, she said only, 'I think you make too little of your generosity, sir, and I am more grateful than I can properly express. The tuition I had from Professor Lowson meant a great deal to me.' She bobbed a curtsy and left the room.

Matthew gazed thoughtfully at the papers on his desk for several minutes. He had avoided the worst pitfalls but, as he had feared, Lucy thought it was he who was paying for her instruction. It was not so. Comfortably off as he was, he could not afford the double burden of the high fees charged by both the professional gentlemen. He had confessed the difficulty when the matter had been raised between Lord Verrell and himself. His lordship had generously offered to pay for both girls, but this the rector would not allow. He had been forced to acknowledge however, that Lucy would be embarrassed if she were told that Verrell was sponsoring her, even if it was presented to her as being no different from the case of the exceptionally clever village boy he was already supporting at Winchester College. There *was* a difference and because of it, reluctant though he was, the rector had agreed to conceal Verrell's generosity towards her.

Verrell fully understood the rector's reluctance. 'A metaphorical hair shirt for you to wear, Rector,' he had said with a crooked smile. 'To "*wear with a difference*", perhaps, like Ophelia's rue?'

He had not waited for a response to that, but had gone on to ask if the rector now knew the reason for Lucy's flight from her temporary employment. Matthew repeated what Lucy had told them and went on to say that the story at Pixham House had been completely reversed. Mrs Montgomery had averred that Lucy had pestered her grandson to notice her, even going so far as to visit his bedroom in the night. It was the young man's threat to reveal her persistence to his grandmother that had driven her from the house.

'Though the lady held it to be true and claimed to feel great indignation on account of it, I suspected that she was less certain than she professed. I met the young man concerned and found myself unable to place any reliance on his word. And so I told Lucy.'

Verrell's grey eyes, wide and clear but unreadable, held his. His voice dry, he said, 'Looking as she does, she is likely to find herself in such a situation again and again. She would do better to look for a husband than for employment. Is there none in view?'

'None I can regard as more than a possibility.'

Verrell did not pursue the subject beyond that point. Afterwards, Matthew had realized, though Verrell recognized the girl's difficulties, he had expressed no sympathy for her. His solution to any future problem she might meet had been put forward with the same cool detachment he had shown before. Even in referring to her musical talent, he had spoken of it as a talent to be valued and nurtured, but as though it were some- thing separate from her; something in her care rather than part of her.

It was strange to Matthew to find himself so drawn towards liking for a man and yet to be uncertain of his true nature. As on the earlier occasion, he concluded that Verrell was a difficult man to understand.

With her new freedom to use Susan's piano and in joyful antici- pation of resuming her musical education, Lucy practised as often and for as long as she felt the Rothwells might find bearable. When the day of their first visit to Tilchester arrived, she and Susan were ready long before the chaise pulled up at the door. Professor Lowson's house was the first to be reached. He had been crippled in a riding accident over twenty years earlier and now aged sixty, was a white-haired, benign martinet. He

122

welcomed Lucy with genuine pleasure, delighted to have a star pupil return to him.

At the end of the two-hour session, when the professor had finished outlining what he wished her to concentrate on before she came to him again, Lucy asked diffidently, 'Professor, would you consider employing me to teach your youngest pupils . . . the beginners?'

'But I do not take any such and those who come new to me my wife instructs in their first term, as perhaps you have forgotten. Apart from that, it would not be at all the thing for you, Miss Daunton.'

'Perhaps you know another teacher who needs someone to teach small children just beginning.'

Looking distressed, he shook his head. 'There are plenty of women in Tilchester competent to do that. For you it would be both harmful and a waste. Would, in the end, destroy your talent. And you would have to be here most days of the week, if not every day. What you could earn even then would not support you. How would you live?'

Swallowing her disappointment, Lucy asked, 'Can I aspire to being a concert pianist then?'

'You have the talent. A year or two more of study and you could appear in ladies' drawing-rooms. But again, it is not for you, so young and so pretty a lady.' He shook his head more agitatedly. 'You cannot know— The uncertainties of such a life before recognition comes. The indignities you might meet with. No, it must not be!'

'It may have to!' Lucy told him doggedly. 'Before long I must find a way to earn my living and whatever the drawbacks I shall have to overcome them.'

As the chaise bore them homeward, half listening to Susan's excited description of the breathing exercises she must do and the tonic sol-fa she must practise, Lucy pondered again over the intractable difficulties facing a young woman needing to earn her own living.

The days passed quietly. By the last week in March the weather began to acknowledge the approach of spring. Susan walked the few hundred yards to the cobbler's cottage to have a buckle secured on one of her shoes and returned with news. The Hammonds of Southways House had come back from their visit to London only to pack for a much longer journey. Mrs Hammond had been diagnosed as in some danger of being consumptive and she and her husband were going to Madeira for a term in the hope that she would receive benefit from a warmer climate. Southways House was to be let as it stood, with all the staff in place – a relief to the village as most were from local homes. Speculation as to the kind of family that might come among them was circulating in the village as briskly as it had before Lord Verrell's arrival at Herriards.

Hardly had Susan dispensed her news when it was put out of mind by the arrival of the younger groom from Herriards to ask if Juba had been seen at the rectory in the past twenty-four hours. He had not and the boy went on to explain that though shut securely into his pen in a loosebox the previous night, in the morning the door had stood ajar and the dog had gone.

'I shut him in meself,' the boy said aggrievedly, 'and I know I shot the bolt, let who will say different. If he's gone, he was stolen, and that I'll hold to.'

The Romanies had gone from Pilgrims' Hollow more than three weeks earlier so rumour could not place the blame on their shoulders. Who else might have stolen the animal was a wonder to all.

As the days passed with no news of the dog's recovery, Lucy

was saddened to think she might never again be assaulted by Juba's determined friendliness. She would, she admitted to herself, positively welcome another mud-spattered gown if Juba could be found.

Succumbing to a chill severe enough to force her to retire to bed, was a matter of peculiar annoyance to Mrs Rothwell because it debarred her from going to the Tilchester Spring Fair held by long custom in the second week in April. It was held in what was known as Priory Field on the outskirts of the town and was renowned for the fine quality of the hams and cheeses offered for sale.

Mrs Rothwell appointed Susan, Lucy and Cook as deputies and entrusted to them a list of purchases to be made and which stalls were to be preferred. Oliffe, the gardener, was to drive them there in the rector's gig.

It was regarded as a treat by all, but especially so by Lucy for whom it would be a first experience.

'Now mind you young ladies keep close to me and to each other and don't go wandering off alone,' admonished Cook, very conscious of her responsibilities as they began to thread their way through the crowd already gathered in Priory Field. Oliffe and the gig had been left to enjoy the hospitality of The Fox and Bacon which overlooked the field.

Three trips back to the inn bearing the burden of their commissioned shopping were necessary before they were free to look around to make small purchases for themselves.

Susan and Cook were deep in a discussion as to which particular hue of some dyed feathers were most suitable for refurbishing Cook's best bonnet when Lucy, standing a little aside from them her gaze roving interestedly over the crowd, saw a small tableau that riveted her attention. The ever-shifting throng shut it off from her almost immediately, but making sure her two companions were still fully occupied, she took a few steps away in the hope of seeing more of what had caught her attention.

Achieving her aim, she stared. Surely the huge, unhappy-looking dog tied to a stout iron stake was Juba! Juba had tan markings on his head and paws, but no white anywhere on him. This dog had a large white bib but no tan. Yet how could there be two so alike in every other way?

There was no mistaking that the two men close to the dog were negotiating a sale and several people had drawn near to listen. Absorbed, suspicious and quite forgetful of Cook's injunctions, Lucy pushed forward to join them.

The possible buyer, a large, middle-aged man with a shrewd expression, looked like a prosperous farmer. The seller was unmistakeably a tinker. Though shorter by a head than the farmer, he was heavily built and had a look of brute strength.

'What I need,' the farmer was saying, 'is a dog that'll not only daunt the foxes, but keep rascally two-legged thieves away from my wife's ducks and hens.'

'Then, sir, as I said, this 'ere chap's just the one for you. 'Eart of a lion and you'd go a long way to find a bigger bug— 'ound anywheres.'

He had thrown out a hand in the dog's direction as he spoke and roused from lethargy, the animal hurled himself towards the offered temptation, his muzzle wrinkling back from a splendid show of gleaming white teeth. The thick cord and the stanchion tethering him both strained but held.

The two men had leapt back. The farmer recovering, frowned. 'Damn it all, man! I've no use for a savage animal that doesn't know his own master.'

'Don't mistake 'im, sir. 'E's a trifle unsettled, belonging as he did to my brother who died suddenlike two weeks since. He's not had time to know me. I'm just trying to make a bit o' cash for the widow, 'im being no use to 'er. Nor to me what 'as 'is own dog. I won't say it'll not take a man to 'andle 'im, but I can't see you having difficulty in that direction.'

'H'mm. . . How much are you asking for him?'

'Well now, you can see he's worth a bit. You won't find 'is like nowhere else neither. I think a fair price would be ten pounds.'

'God bless my soul! I could buy a donkey for that.'

'Well, 'e ain't far short of that size. He's young, sound, and whole. He'll father good pups on the right bitch and pay for 'isself in no time.'

'I'll give you five,' said the farmer firmly.

The tinker shook his head. 'It wouldn't be doing right by my sister-in-law—'

But the dog had caught a familiar scent. His eyes searched the crowd, found Lucy. Raising his massive head he implored her sympathy, howling his misery at the pains and indignities of recent days.

It was Juba! Lucy was sure of it now despite the white bib. But girls did not accost strange men, especially in such a place as a fair, and it was with thumping heart that she stepped forward.

'I beg your pardon, sir,' she said to the farmer, 'but before you proceed, I have to tell you the dog is not this man's to sell.'

The farmer stared in astonishment, taking in her charming grey muslin gown, neat blue pelisse and bonnet. 'What makes you say that, missy?' he asked.

'I know him. He belongs to Lord Verrell who has had people looking for him everywhere for more than two weeks.'

The tinker glared ferociously at Lucy. 'Don't you listen to her, sir! This couldn't be no lord's dog. Me brother had 'im six months and more agone.' He thrust his snarling, yellow-toothed face closer to her. 'What's your game, eh? Coming 'ere blackening an honest man's name!'

Lucy was forced to step back and the tinker pushed in between her and Juba though keeping a nervous distance from the dog's eager jaws.

Appealing to the farmer, Lucy said, 'The dog's appearance has been altered, but if I could handle him a moment I could very soon prove we are acquainted.'

The dog's straining efforts to reach Lucy was dragging the stanchion further from the ground and the farmer said doubtfully, 'I don't know that it would be safe—'

The tinker laughed nastily. 'You want to be torn to pieces . . . 'ave your pretty looks spoiled?' He swung back to the farmer. 'I ask you, sir, what's a young mort like 'er doing 'ere alone if she's not up to something? No better than she ought to be, I'll take my oath!'

But in the brief moment the man's attention had turned away from her, Lucy had dodged round him to be engulfed in the disguised Juba's ecstatic greeting. When she could free a hand, she put it against the white bib and the stiffness of the patch told its own story.

'This white – it's paint!' she called to the farmer 'Feel here . . . and here where he should have brown markings.'

Big man though he was, the farmer hesitated.

'It's quite safe. He is very friendly, truly he is, unless he thinks you mean him harm,' Lucy assured him.

The farmer ventured near enough to touch a cautious hand to Juba's head. Finding it tolerated, he ventured further to feel the white patch under the dog's chin. The next moment he swung round to demand wrathfully, 'Where's that scoundrelly tinker? I'll have the constable to him!'

But the tinker, with the wisdom of his kind, had already slunk away into the crowd.

Only too pleased to have escaped becoming the possessor of

128

stolen goods, at Lucy's request, the farmer used his pocket knife to sever the cord holding Juba and handed her the end. 'Will he go peaceable with you, miss? He could have you over in a trice.'

'He already has on one occasion,' Lucy laughed, but I think he's too anxious to be home to be other than biddable now.'

'And where might his home be?'

'He lives at Chalworth, as I do.'

The farmer frowned. 'But that's five miles off! What are you doing alone at a fair, missy?'

Lucy clasped her hand to her mouth in alarmed recollection. 'Oh, but I'm not. Cook and Susan will be worried to death wondering where I am!'

'So I should think! We'd best find them as quick as maybe. Where's a likely place to start?'

'The inn, I should think. We made it a rendezvous point and the gig's there. But, sir, I cannot put you to the trouble of accompanying me.'

'The least I can do after you saved me from being cozened by that tinker. Not that I didn't suspicion him,' he added, for his pride's sake. 'But Josiah Jepson don't take kindly to being took for a fool. I'll see you safe to your friends young lady. You and – what name did you say the dog goes by?'

'Juba.'

'Funny sort of name for a dog. But then, lords and such incline to the fanciful. Which lord is it owns him?'

'Lord Verrell, Baron Farleton. He'll be delighted to have Juba back, I'm sure.'

Reaching The Fox and Bacon, they found an agitated group just returned from searching the fairground for the missing member of its party. It took several minutes to pacify a tearful Cook, but at last explanations and exclamations at an end, there arose the problem of how to convey the enlarged party home in a gig already made less commodious by numerous bulky parcels. Susan's nervousness of Juba had also to be taken into account.

Farmer Jepson solved the problem by offering to convey half the party to its destination in his own gig, declaring it no trouble at all. So with Cook as chaperon, Lucy and Juba travelled with Mr Jepson, while Oliffe drove Susan and explanations to the rectory.

CHAPTER THIRTEEN

Having decided that Lucy could safely be driven the length of the village street in the farmer's company with Juba as her protector, Cook asked to be set down at the rectory gates.

Herriards' tall, wrought-iron gates had recently been painted and were looking very handsome. Mr Jepson was visibly impressed, Lucy saw. He had brought the conversation round to *lords* and their ways so often during the journey from Tilchester she felt she could not do less than give him the pleasure of driving up to the house and perhaps being thanked by Lord Verrell himself for having driven so far out of his way.

Had she come alone to Herriards she would have taken Juba to the stables and given him to the groom or stable boy and hoped to slip away unseen by anyone in the house. Mr Jepson straightened up his solid form and seemed almost to swell as they passed along the drive and pulled up before the fine old house, which told Lucy she was doing the right thing.

The farmer was fated not to have his full reward however. Lord Verrell was away from home Penfold told Lucy when he opened the door to her. She asked for Mrs Gresham who came into the hall at once. Told the farmer had come five miles out of his way and why, she at once agreed to say a few words to him and went out to the gig. Finding him a pleasant, unassuming man, she invited him to come into the house to take some refreshment before driving home. His red face shining with delight, Mr Jepson climbed down from his gig even while proclaiming that so much was entirely unnecessary.

Juba was despatched to the stables to be fed and groomed and Mrs Gresham ushered her two guests into his lordship's drawing-room to Mr Jepson's great gratification. There, his hostess soon had him at ease with a tankard of excellent, locally brewed ale at his elbow and the double assurance that his lordship valued his dog and would be sorry to have missed the opportunity to thank Mr Jepson for his part in the recovery. His lordship, she said, had travelled into Surrey the previous day to settle some problem on his estate there and was unlikely to return before two or three more days had passed.

The farmer was an honest man and would not take more credit than was his due. 'I had no more to do with the dog's recovery than to bring him home,' he said. ' 'Twas the little lady what truly found him and saved me paying out good money to a rogue.' He told her the full story then, making much of Lucy's courage and good sense.

Lucy, unable to stem the tide, rose to her feet as soon as was possible without discourtesy, saying it was past time for her to return to the rectory. Reluctantly, but gallantly, Mr Jepson rose too and claimed the honour of driving her there. Mrs Gresham accompanied them to the door of the house and again assured them of Lord Verrell's gratitude and his undoubted wish to express his thanks for Juba's recovery.

Anxious to know if Juba was recovering his spirits and remembering Mrs Gresham had said Lord Verrell was to be away for two or three more days, Lucy walked back to Herriards the following afternoon and went straight to the stables.

Naylor, the head groom, was in the yard and told her the dog was feeling a trifle sorry for himself. 'He hasn't liked having the paint cleaned out of his coat, but I attended to it myself and it says a lot for his good nature that he never once showed his teeth to me.' Frowning, he added indignantly, 'That tinker! He must have given the poor beast more than one beating. You can feel the stripes under his coat and he's lost weight, too.'

He opened the door to Juba's pen for Lucy, and the dog, though he rose a little stiffly from his bed of straw, greeted his visitor as warmly if less boisterously than usual. His colouring was his own again, though his coat looked somewhat the worse for wear. Lucy sat down on a bale of hay to murmur comfortingly to him and pet him with gentle hands.

'He'll take all you can give him of that, miss,' Naylor told her with a smile and left her to it.

There was a strong smell of the liniment with which Juba's weals had been treated and she suspected that some of the reek would transfer to her own clothes. She was sure of it when the dog flopped down and putting his large head in her lap, gazed soulfully into her eyes and sighed for past sorrows.

'Well, my poor boy, I think you may have discovered that the world is not always a friendly place,' she told him with wry sympathy. 'Though how a large fellow like yourself was taken into captivity, I cannot think. I hope you have learned not to be too trusting.'

She sat for some time idly fondling his ears and murmuring sympathy for his past tribulations. Occasionally, footsteps crossed the yard outside the loosebox as the two grooms and the stable-boy went about their work. She took no more notice of the last than the first and was unaware of the man who stood looking in over the open top half of the door for several minutes.

133

Presently, opening the lower door, he walked in and said, 'I have my people scouring the countryside for that scapegrace hound for days on end without success. Then I am absent only two days and return to find him here undeservedly being made much of.'

Lucy rose in a startled flurry from her seat. 'My lord! You were not expected.'

'Was I not? I do tend to come and go as I please.' He stood looking at her, smiling in a way she had not seen before. It made him look younger and in some way different. When she did not speak, he went on, 'Naylor tells me I have you to thank for wresting the useless animal from the hands of a rascally tinker.'

'Nothing so dramatic,' she disclaimed hurriedly, his unexpected appearance embarrassing her as though she had been caught in some misbehaviour. 'All I did was tell the farmer who was on the point of buying him that Juba was not the tinker's to sell.'

'Oh, is that all? And of course, confronting tinkers and unknown farmers at country fairs is an everyday matter to you!'

With no one else was she so frequently tongue-tied and uncertain of herself. Uselessly wishing she had not relied on Mrs Gresham's statement regarding his absence, she stood in vaguely defensive silence, wishing above all that she had not come.

Juba had climbed to his feet and now nudged Verrell for attention, but intent on the girl before him Verrell did no more than give him a perfunctory pat on the head.

His smile had dimmed a little. 'Do not belittle the service rendered, Miss Daunton. Believe me grateful and allow me to thank you as you deserve.'

Lucy said awkwardly, 'Well, it was no great thing I did, really. And now I should be going.'

'But you will come back to the house first to say goodbye to Mrs Gresham? She will be expecting you, I am sure.'

134

Lucy flushed. Belatedly she realized she was trespassing. She no longer had the right to come to Herriards' stables as and when she chose. More awkwardly still, she said, 'I have not visited the house. I just slipped in to see how Juba was doing.'

Something flashed in his eyes, but all he said was, 'Well, you will come in now, will you not?'

'Oh, no! I mean, no thank you. I do not wish to impose on Mrs Gresham.'

There was a lengthy pause before he said drily, 'I see. Another day perhaps?' No vestige of a smile remained. He looked to her as grim as ever he had.

'Yes, of course.' She brushed straws from her gown, wishing he would move aside instead of standing where he was between her and the door. She made a further small show of patting Juba's head in farewell, saying, 'Goodbye, old fellow. Be good.' She looked up. Verrell had not moved and did not move, but now his scowling gaze was turned on Juba and she jerked out worriedly, 'You will not punish him for his absence, will you? The tinker thrashed him several times your groom says.'

He made a small exasperated sound in his throat and brought an angry glittering gaze up to hers. 'How I treat my dog is my own affair, wouldn't you say, Miss Daunton? I am as little likely to take instruction on the matter of my behaviour as are you. But before I remove myself and my unwanted gratitude, which is so obviously what you most desire, perhaps it might be as well if we bring into the open what it is that colours our every exchange. Even a simple acknowledgement of obligation.'

His leap into anger startled her. Far from wanting to provoke it all she wanted to do was escape. Before she could say anything, he swept on, his voice coldly incisive.

'As you once pointed out, nothing can alter the fact that you are your father's daughter. Add to that I made an impression on

135

you at our first meeting that time has done nothing to change. From those things, I suppose it follows quite naturally that you expect no good of me. So accepting what is impossible of amendment, I will save you day to day anxiety by engaging to give you prior warning when I am ready to indulge the vengefulness you look for from me. Until that time you may be easy. But when the occasion arises, I promise you you will have cause to remember it.' His last words were spoken with a soft and venomous violence that shocked. He followed them with a brief, brilliant and utterly unnerving smile, turned and walked out of the loosebox.

Chilled and shaking, Lucy stood listening to his footsteps fade into distance. If she could have found sufficient command over her trembling legs, she would have run from the stables and down the carriageway. Only her overpowering wish to get away from Herriards at last set her moving out of the loosebox, across the yard and down towards the road.

Once outside the gates she halted, her pounding heart almost suffocating her. Closing her eyes, she lived over again the last grievous minutes before Verrell had walked away from her. *How* had it come to that? She called up his smiling entry and the friendly tone of his first remarks; remembered her own foolish, maladroit responses. Had it been her awkwardness, her doubts, fears and sense of guilt, ending in that witless plea for Juba not to be punished, that had wrenched the final baleful threat from him? What had he *ever* done to make her think that he would treat Juba harshly? He had taken pity on an abandoned pup in a foreign country and brought him back to this one. Juba showed a healthy respect for his orders but no fear of him. The idea that what *she* said and did might have some influence on his words and actions took hold. To meet with the constant expectation of unkindness where none was intended must provoke the easiest-going man alive. And *that* Lord Verrell was not!

She opened her eyes and began walking towards the rectory. But then, as always, she came back to why he had chosen to come to live in Chalworth and buy Herriards. It was what had first put the idea of vengefulness into her mind; that and the way he had behaved towards her at their first meeting. Yet he had taken her in when Hyram Smith had carried her to Herriards and even if Mrs Gresham had been chiefly responsible for that and the care she was given, it must have been with his acquiescence.

There was too, the fact that she was benefiting from his provision of a conveyance to take her and Susan to Tilchester each week. Though she did not doubt the provision was made as a compliment to the rector and therefore principally for Susan's benefit, her share of it could not be ignored. It placed her in his debt.

Thoughts and feelings were in bewildering confusion: she could be sure of nothing and could decide nothing.

Julia Gresham took one look at her nephew's expression when he entered the smaller parlour where she was sitting and said, 'Oh dear! Did your business at Mardens Hall not prosper?'

For a moment it looked as though Verrell had not understood what she said, then with a shake of his head he said, 'Oh, it went well enough. I've left what remains to be done in good hands. I returned early because of Juba and as soon as I rode in Naylor met me with the news that he was back. I went into his pen to look at him.'

He was slow to add to that and she prompted, 'Has something happened? Is he unwell?'

'No. It's nothing do with Juba. Miss Daunton was there.'

'Was she? I did not know. She has not called at the house.'

'So she said.' His tone was sour, his expression dark, and

darker still when he added, 'And now will not because *I* am here.'

'She could not have *said* that!'

'She had no need. She made it plain without saying so. Dammit, Julia, I know I behaved badly at our first meeting but she will neither forgive nor forget.'

'It was not long ago you yourself told me neither was easy to do.'

'Did I? Yes. Well . . .' He shrugged that aside to pursue his grievance. 'Whenever she looks at me with those great dark eyes of hers I see myself reflected in them as a Macbeth come fresh from the murder of Duncan. One would think it was her father who was wronged and *I* the culprit! Today, not for the first time, she begged me not to punish Juba for his absence as though she suspects I regularly beat my dogs and probably my horses, too. I tell you, I could throttle her!'

'I take it you did not,' Julia said with dark amusement. 'But by the way you are prowling up and down I suspect you did *something*. So please stand still for a moment and tell me what you did do?'

'She rouses the very devil in me . . . a devil I never suspected myself of harbouring until I met her.'

'That's the excuse. What did you do?'

He ended his restless walk to look down at her and to say almost belligerently, 'Oh, nothing more than to inform her that when I was ready to revenge myself on her I would give her due warning. To which I added the promise that it would be memorable.'

'And you said it very convincingly no doubt.' Julia's voice held no amusement now only a flat exasperated resignation.

'Oh yes. Attila the Hun at his most impressive. I attacked her as an equal . . . as an adversary. And she no more than a child! You don't need to point it out.'

'Then I shall not. But tell me, Harry . . . are you certain there is no secret wish in you to visit her father's sins on her?'

'No. Good God, *no*! What a cowardly villain that would make me! But there is something about the girl that bedevils me. Something that drives me over the edge of reason. There you have it.'

But even as he spoke he wondered if, after all, there was not deep within him some dark, atavistic sense that waited only opportunity to be loosed to stalk, hunt and finally destroy Lucy Daunton. He shook his head, uncertain of what it was he was denying, saw Julia's troubled look and said, 'I have been too often and for too long in coarse company. I learned the hard way that if I was given a blow to strike back at once and twice as hard. It became instinctive.'

Whatever his problems were, Julia thought, only he could solve them. She said, 'Let it go, Harry, for the present. What you need just now is a drink. Ring for Penfold and then come and sit down and tell me about the Mardens Hall business.'

CHAPTER FOURTEEN

By the middle of May, Mrs Gresham decided she could now use to advantage the acquaintance she had made in the village and an evening party of respectable size could be given. The four members of the rector's household were among the first to receive their invitations and when all had been sent, no one in Chalworth who had been invited declined to come unless compelled by what they considered the unkindest of circumstances.

To Lucy, the event loomed as a greater ordeal than her first visit to the home she had lost had been. In the weeks that had passed since Lord Verrell had spoken the demoralizing words that haunted her memory, she had not been in his company. How was she to meet him with anything approaching normal composure? She had told the Rothwells nothing of what had happened and could think of no excuse good enough to allow her to avoid accompanying them to Herriards.

When they came together on the evening of the party, Mrs Rothwell remarked on her silence. She excused it by claiming a slight headache. The Rothwells' intention had been that they should walk the short distance to Herriards, but anticipating this,

Lord Verrell had informed them that a carriage would be sent to bring them. Entering it, Lucy felt very much akin to one of the unfortunate French aristocrats entering a tumbrel and what courage she had been able to muster lost ground.

Their welcome was what, in a less nervous state, she might have expected it to be: they were greeted by their host and hostess with a warmth and courtesy that embraced the whole party. Lucy managed to curtsy, smile and say what she should, but it was with a deep breath of relief that she passed with the others into the larger drawing-room to mingle with the guests already arrived.

When the last had come, there were fifty or more. Country dances had been promised for the younger people, cards and conversation for their elders. Supper was to be at eight o'clock, a time Mrs Gresham judged suited local custom and the majority of those present.

The first hour or two passed uneventfully. Lucy danced, talked, was congratulated by Mrs Gresham on renewing her musical studies with Professor Lowson and, since her host did not approach her individually during this time, gradually relaxed. But then he did.

She had just moved away from a gossiping group of young people and was standing looking to see where any of the Rothwells were when she saw Verrell coming towards her. Resisting the impulse to hurry in the opposite direction, she waited. He stood in silence for a moment looking down at her, his expression unreadable. Then, quietly, he said, 'I thought you would like to know, Miss Daunton, that Juba is now quite recovered from his misfortunes, but he is being kept on a tighter rein than formerly and given small chance to roam. He feels his loss of freedom and would, I'm sure, welcome a visit from a friend. If you would care to visit him in his pen, he is usually there in the early afternoons when the grooms are at their dinner. No one else will intrude upon you while you are there, I give you my word.'

Surprised by this approach, Lucy, did not immediately answer and he prompted a little sharply, 'You will come?'

Now because she must answer and could not face argument, Lucy forced a 'yes' and 'thank you' past her lips.

'Good.' He nodded at her and walked away before she could add anything else to her agreement. Confused, Lucy stared after him, wondering in what spirit he had made the invitation. A step down from the baleful promise he had made her? Or merely a prop to the appearance of normality that was to be preserved between them until that promise was fulfilled? Of course she would not go! Never again would she visit Herriards unless circumstances compelled her, as tonight.

Watching him making his slow way through his guests, she was surprised to be swept by a wave of tiredness: not physical tiredness, but a weariness of the mind, heart, spirit. With sudden passion, she longed for an end to the recurring friction between them; wished with all her heart that there was no past to trouble them; that Lord Verrell was no more than an ordinary acquaintance whom she could meet on even ground and without stress. A useless wish, as she knew.

Among the guests were the brother and sister who had taken Southways House for a year. Miss Tarrant, vaguely fortyish, was the elder by some ten or twelve years. Julia Gresham had called on her and found her a gentle, nervous woman. Meeting her brother two days later in someone else's house, she was struck by the similarity of their looks and their utter dissimilarity in every other respect. He was about Harry's age, perhaps a little younger, not handsome but with looks that stayed in the mind. It appeared to her a very *knowledgeable* face; the eyes more green than grey and keenly perceptive, the thoughts behind them subtle and secret. A sophisticated man with a sharp intelligence cloaked by velvet charm, she thought. But what interested her most was the formidable strength of will she sensed underlying all: Mr Tarrant, she was certain, was a man who let little stand in his way of getting what he wanted.

The gentleman's presence tonight was especially pleasing to local mamas with unmarried daughters, for not only was he a personable man with a sister to keep house for him who could be called on, but rumour had it that he was rich.

Richard Tarrant himself, having deftly extricated himself from a frontal attack by a lady with three daughters in want of husbands, was looking round trying to decide where next to direct his steps when his gaze fell on the very pretty girl to whom he had been introduced early in the evening. However, making his way towards her, he found himself pre-empted by his host. Tarrant almost turned away but something in the purposefulness of Verrell's approach and the sudden tensing of the girl's slight figure held his attention

He knew as much as was locally current of the Daunton/Verrell story and now, intrigued by the possibility of some mischievous twist to the tale, he drew to one side to watch the pair. Their meeting was brief: the man spoke, the girl stayed silent; the man spoke again and when he had done the girl's lips shaped an obviously reluctant *yes*. And that was all.

Tarrant had not been near enough to hear what was said, but his gaze lingered on Miss Daunton, interested to see if she might yet show some final response to whatever had passed between the two. Though she held her expression to careful neutrality as she watched Verrell pass among his guests, the knuckles of the hand holding her fan gleamed white. Whatever the girl had given consent to, Tarrant was certain her mind had rejected. And now, just for a moment, her shoulders sagged as though under a weight that sapped her strength. His interest deepened. When her figure straightened and her head lifted, he recognized the gallantry in the action and moved quickly to close the remaining distance between them.

When Verrell thought himself far enough away from Lucy Daunton to escape notice, he turned and looked back. She was no longer alone he saw. The Hammonds' recently arrived tenant had joined her and she was laughing. Laughing, and looking as carefree as she should look at her age. Laughter was not something he had ever evoked from her. When had he attempted it? Her agreement to visit Juba had been dragged out of her. What had she made of his invitation? Had it done anything to reduce the brutal, razor-sharp edges of his last words to her when he had left her in Juba's pen? Or diminished by the smallest degree the prejudice that he and her father between them had created in her?

It was ridiculous that so young and untried an innocent should repeatedly – and with ease – unsettle him, throw him out of his stride. Simply by being herself.

Twenty minutes later he saw that Miss Daunton and Tarrant were still together, had found seats in a quiet corner and were in animated conversation. Though the man was a stranger, she was having no difficulty conversing with *him*, he thought, his mouth twisting. If matters progressed from such a favourable beginning, the young blade who visited the rectory from time to time might need to look to his laurels if he had serious intentions towards the girl.

CHAPTER FIFTEEN

A few days after the evening party at Herriards, Lucy was surprised to receive a note from Miss Tarrant inviting her to take tea with her on the following day or, if that was not convenient, to name another. After consulting Mrs Rothwell, she returned a note accepting the invitation for the suggested occasion.

Southways House was one of the older houses in Chalworth and, after Herriards, the largest. Built to face south, it presented only a side wall to the village street from which it was not separated even by as much as a row of railings. This wall showed two rows of three high windows and under them the barred demi-lunes of its kitchens and offices which were semi-basement. Because of this, the windows of the principal rooms were high enough above the street not to permit being looked into by passers-by. The main entrance was in the long south-facing wall and was approached by a short gravelled drive beyond which lay the stables, coachhouse and gardens.

A little puzzled by the interest shown in her by a lady of more than forty to whom she had only spoken briefly at the Herriards' evening party, Lucy presented herself at Southways House in good time on the appointed day and was shown into the drawing-room.

Miss Tarrant rose from her chair by a comfortable log fire and advanced to greet her guest a little fussily but with every appearance of genuine pleasure.

Taking a seat opposite her, Lucy wondered what interests they might find they shared. Like Mrs Gresham, she had noticed that Miss Tarrant's features lacked the force that made her brother's both attractive and interesting. The lady appeared negative to his positive.

For all that, she was an attentive hostess and a pleasant, if boring companion, her conversation strolling along well-trodden paths.

It was a surprise to Lucy to discover eventually that Miss Tarrant usually accompanied her brother to the different countries to which his interests took him. Believing her hostess must have a store of interesting stories to tell, she did her best to lead her into recounting some of them. Miss Tarrant however, seemed to have difficulty even to say what influenced her brother's journeying. It was more the uncertainty of not understanding than any wish to conceal his purposes, Lucy decided. There might have been some clue in the Tarrants frequently being guests in embassies or governmental houses, but Lucy was unable to read it.

'How I envy you!' she said. 'To have travelled so far and seen so much. You must find a great deal of enjoyment in it.'

'Oh, *no!*' For once Miss Tarrant's tone was positive. 'It is not at all comfortable arriving in strange places – strange *countries* – where the servants have difficulty understanding what one wants and one dare not venture out for fear of being robbed or set upon. And everything so strange. Even the food not at all what one is used to. And frequently so hot! The climate, I mean. I think Jamaica was the worst. Always lizards on the walls inside the house and snakes outside in the garden! And the snakes tried to get into the house too and quite often succeeded.'

She regarded Lucy dolefully, shaking her head again. 'You have no idea, my dear, what it is like to see none but black or yellow faces around one, or faces that are otherwise singular in their appearance. Or to be constantly in fear of the people rising in rebellion as they did in San Domingo.' As a last comically tragic observation, she added, 'There were snakes in India, too.'

Trying not to smile, Lucy asked, 'Was there nothing you enjoyed?'

'Nothing I remember.' The older woman stared unhappily into the fire, murmuring half to herself, 'I live in dread of where Richard's next start will take him. It is all to do with the government, but I do not know what.' She lifted her head sharply to look at Lucy and said worriedly, 'You will not tell him I said so? He thinks me enough of a sad shatterbrain.'

Hiding her surprise, Lucy said reassuringly, 'No, indeed.' She had thought of suggesting to Miss Tarrant that she tell her brother she did not wish to accompany him on his next journey, but thought better of it and changed the subject. Miss Tarrant, she suspected, was incapable of saying *no*.

She was ready to take her leave when Richard Tarrant came into the room. Expressing surprise to see her and regret that she was on the point of returning to the rectory and could not be persuaded to delay, he at once offered his escort. With his grey-green eyes showing such smiling pleasure in looking at her, it did not occur to her make any of the demurs she had once made to Lord Verrell.

From Southways House to the rectory was no more than three or four hundred yards. Even over that short distance, conversation had an ease and rapidity that Lucy had been unable to find with his sister. It had been like that at Herriards when they first met, she remembered.

147

On the rectory doorstep he declined her invitation to come in, saying, 'There is a business matter at Southways awaiting my attention that must not wait longer. But you will say all that is proper for me.' His eyes twinkled at her in a way that told her that in *her* case the delay had been readily made. He did not prolong the parting, but simply bowed over her hand and was gone very briskly.

Waiting for the door to be opened, Lucy wondered if his surprise at finding her with his sister had been quite genuine: it seemed to her he had appeared very promptly upon the servant being rung for to show her out. If it had been a deliberate manoeuvre she saw no reason to be displeased.

Following a second invitation from Miss Tarrant two weeks later, the pattern was repeated, except that on this occasion Richard made no pretence at being surprised to find Lucy with his sister.

June came in on a burst of fine weather. By this time the houses that were to replace those in Slippy-Slosh Lane were nearing completion. Throughout their building their gradual rise had been watched by those destined to occupy them. The emotions they expressed ranged widely, extending from a cantankerous determination to resist being moved at all, to an almost tearful eagerness for the time of possession.

It was now that Peter Eddis came to make his long-delayed stay at Herriards. Any chance of shooting was over except for attempting a pigeon or two, but Sir Peter had other interests in Chalworth. He called at the rectory the first day after his arrival and was received with quiet pleasure.

In the second week of his stay, Mrs Gresham proposed for his entertainment a picnic party to the Sussex Downs. The ladies of the rectory enthusiastically seconded the idea when it was put to them and and plans quickly went forward. An invitation to the Tarrants to join the party was also accepted with pleasure. Responsibility for the contents of the picnic hampers was divided between Mrs Gresham, Mrs Rothwell and their cooks. The provision of suitable transport for them all was passed to the gentlemen.

They were fortunate in their choice of day. They set out in pleasant warmth and brightness and found the air sweet with the scents of summer. To save the horses a steep climb they travelled a leafy roundabout route. Trees were still in their first light green and bronze leaf, the colours vibrant against the blue of the sky. Their destination was the beacon hill known as the Trundle on the Duke of Richmond's estate from where they might expect clear views over some of the loveliest Sussex countryside.

Two carriages carried the ladies, the gentlemen rode and a Herriards' wagon brought two servants, chairs for the older ladies and the hampers. The vehicles were quickly ranged neatly on one side of their picnic site and the horses, relieved of harness and saddle, were tethered where they could nibble the thyme-scented grass. While this was done, Lucy stood at gaze. The view north was fully as beautiful as she had been led to expect, but looking south, the flat land there was bounded by the sea and this was her first glimpse of it. She gazed at it entranced. A dazzling reflection of the sun, it lay some ten or twelve miles distant, a sheet of gold that had no horizon but simply lost itself in the sky. She longed to be nearer, to see at close hand that tantalizing golden expanse.

Only when she sensed that people were beginning to dispose themselves in a semi-circle about the crown of the hill did she turn away and choose a place for herself on the grass at sufficient distance from Susan and Peter Eddis – so clearly engrossed in each other – not to allow them to think they must talk to her.

Immediately, as though this was what he had waited for, Richard Tarrant went to sit beside her.

He had been watching her drinking in the seaward view, delighting in her delight, yet pricked by an amused contempt for himself, an unwillingness to believe he was on the way to being captivated by her. His interest had begun in half mischievous curiosity, but unexpectedly, it had both changed and grown. It would not last of course; there was little likelihood of the attention of such a seasoned campaigner as himself being held for long by the charms of a girl so young and inexperienced. A quick mind allied to a sweet innocence and a delightful little figure were not enough for lasting interest. But while it did last, he saw no bar to his setting up a mild flirtation with her to enliven his stay in Chalworth and perhaps flatter a girlish vanity in doing so. He intended her no harm. The worst that could befall her was perhaps a slight melancholy when he departed or found another interest. He had no fear of danger to himself, a surfeit of her company would wear out her charm for him.

It was left to Lord Verrell to sit beside the one stranger among them. Mrs Rothwell had invited a recently widowed friend and neighbour to join the expedition, but a painful attack of rheumatism had forced her to confess herself unable to come. She had begged Mrs Rothwell to take in her place the young niece who had come to stay with her for a few weeks and who was finding the first few days rather dull. Miss Wynn was a pretty young woman of twenty years, with a cloud of fluffy blonde hair, large light-blue eyes and a pale skin. She had, too, a pretty and curvaceous figure and a breathless manner of speaking. She was also endowed with just enough vanity to enable her to think Lord Verrell sat with her from choice rather than as a matter of courtesy.

The value of opportunity had been pointed out to her by her

mama and she chattered happily to his lordship, fluttering long lashes and receiving anything he said with dazzling smiles and instant agreement. Treatment, which in very short time, brought Verrell to the edge of murder.

Hearing Richard Tarrant laugh, Verrell's gaze lifted to him and his partner and wished there could be an exchange. He would prefer to have Miss Daunton's tart rejoinders sting his ears than continue to listen to the syrupy compliments dripping from the lips of the *claqueur* at his side. Moreover, he reminded himself, he had unfinished business with Miss Daunton.

As far as he knew she had not yet availed herself of his invitation to visit Juba and he was impatient to tax her with it. More importantly, he was impatient to rid his conscience of the burden of what he had said to her in Juba's pen.

He had mentioned this intention to Julia, who had said, 'I think you should. But remember to tread softly and speak gently, Harry, even if you do not immediately receive the response you look for. Put a guard on your temper and keep in mind that you are hoping to conciliate . . . to *please*.' She him given him a glinting smile. 'Don't tell me you don't know how to charm a woman. You've wasted some of your talent on me when you've had an object to serve.'

It was sound advice, he knew. The trouble was, where Lucy Daunton was concerned, guarding his temper was oddly difficult, as past experience had shown. He was given no opportunity to make any attempt at it on this occasion. Richard Tarrant had so thoroughly established himself as Miss Daunton's companion for the duration of the outing, not only engrossing her attention but also appearing to find considerable enjoyment in doing so that Verrell could do nothing but watch them with increasing annoyance and something very like envy.

It had been slowly dawning on Miss Wynn that she had less

than her companion's full attention and jumping to her feet, she exclaimed, 'Do come and look at the beautiful view behind us, Lord Verrell. As a stranger to Sussex, I should like so much to have someone knowledgeable point out the various features.'

Clutching his arm, she pulled him in the direction she had indicated. The ground was uneven and on the way, taking a carefully careless step while gazing up into his face, she gave a small shriek and tumbled down a slight declivity which took her out of sight of the rest of the company. Silently cursing her, Verrell strode down after her.

Their attention drawn by the girl's cry, Sir Peter and the rector hurried to see if help was needed, but Verrell appeared almost at once carrying Miss Wynn. Her arm about his neck and her head lolling against his shoulder, she had all the appearance of someone who had taken a dreadful fall instead of a topple down a slight, grassy slope.

Carrying her to where the older ladies sat, Verrell set her down in the nearest vacant chair and gave her into their care. Dutifully, he remained to see her come to her senses if not to sense and then at Mrs Gresham's request, went to procure a glass of wine from the wagon for her.

Mrs Gresham had a shrewd idea of what had been happening and of Verrell's mood. Taking the wine from him, to Miss Wynn's chagrin, she said, 'Thank you. I think Miss Wynn should rest now, so leave her with us.' She nodded dismissal and thankfully, he took it.

Lucy had watched the small pantomime and taken the impression that it was much ado about nothing. She could not say what made her suspect Miss Wynn's fall had been designed and her subsequent faintness entirely spurious, but she felt strongly that what would be most conducive to the young lady's speedy recovery was a good shaking. The harshness of her judgement surprised her. What did it matter to her if Miss Wynn was doing her best to awaken Lord Verrell's interest? She turned back to Tarrant and was immediately struck by a quite different thought.

Her expression caused his eyebrows to quirk suspiciously. 'I see a question in your big brown eyes, Miss Daunton.'

Lucy laughed, her dimples coming into play in a way that delighted Tarrant. 'I am wondering why you alone of the gentlemen did not rush to Miss Wynn's aid as the others did,' she quizzed him.

'I never waste effort. I should have been as redundant as were they,' he said blandly. 'Even less do I choose to interfere with the pleasures of others.' His gaze drifted to Verrell who was now deeply and thankfully engaged in conversation with the rector. 'Especially when they outrank me.' He brought his gaze back to Lucy, his smile almost feline. 'Besides, I was not Miss Wynn's target. Nor is she mine.'

The gleam in his eyes told Lucy who was. Not for the first time, he was flirting with her and she was enjoying it. It was very different from Robin's awkward, blurted utterances. Though she took none of it seriously, it lifted her spirits. Having a sophisticated man such as Mr Tarrant choose to spend time with her could not be other than flattering. Apart from that, she liked him, liked his readiness to smile, liked his self-mockery. She was comfortable with him and had begun to look on him as a friend.

Later, journeying homeward, Tarrant reviewed the past two or three hours and allowed himself to recognize that so far Lucy Daunton's attractions had not begun to pall. They might even have strengthened their pull a little. But it was early days.

Verrell's mood was less complacent.

CHAPTER SIXTEEN

On the following morning, Sir Peter came to keep an appointment made with the rector in the course of the picnic. The two men spent half an hour secluded in the rector's study, the rector then emerged alone and putting his head round the sitting-room door, called Susan to him.

His serious expression brought instant alarm to Susan's face and she rose slowly from her seat as though fearful of going to him. When she reached him however, he smiled, bent to kiss her forehead and said quietly, 'He's in the study, my dear, waiting to say all that you already know. Go and be made happy.'

'Oh, Papa!' was all Susan could manage in a choked voice. She threw her arms around his neck, kissed his cheek and hurried past him.

Seating himself in his usual chair, the rector met his wife's eager gaze and nodded at her, 'Yes, my dear, you were perfectly right. He is a sensible, pleasant young man and Susan will have things as much her own way as you do.'

'Enough but not too much,' Mrs Rothwell said serenely and smiled down at her sewing.

Fifteen minutes later, the young couple joined them with happy conscious faces. Lucy added her congratulations to what Susan's parents said, but could not avoid feeling a small pang of envy for the other girl's settled future.

The Midsummer Ball at the Ashwick Assembly Rooms came close upon the heels of this event. Tickets for it had already been bought and it was decided that Herriards and the rectory should make one party to attend.

Two days before it, Robin and Jane came. It had been many weeks since their last visit and, as time passed, Lucy had come to feel that the friendship between them was growing thin. Not, perhaps, on Robin's part but on Jane's. This visit seemed to confirm it. It was short and Jane was quiet and moody. Before they left, in a few moments when she and Lucy were alone together, she said almost sulkily, 'I cannot continue to come here, Lucy. It grows ever more difficult. I know Grandmama does not wish it and if she finds out we have been deceiving her she would be so angry and we should all suffer for it, including Mama. It is all very well for Robin to say he will do as he chooses but it is not so easy for me.'

'No, of course you must not come if it makes you unhappy and uncomfortable,' Lucy said. 'But I shall be sorry to lose your friend-ship.'

'Yes, well—' was Jane's response to that. She expressed no regrets, which told Lucy that friendship between them was indeed dead and another door to her old life had closed.

As it happened, Matthew was unable to accompany his family to the ball. An elderly and sick parishioner took a turn for the worse and a late message begged the comfort of the rector's presence and his prayers for the dying woman.

Entering the ballroom, Lucy could not help remembering the disasters of her first visit. She wondered if Lord Verrell remembered, too, and looking towards him, found him gazing at her in a grave considering way. A blush coloured her cheeks and hurriedly, she turned her gaze away.

Dancing was to begin with a cotillion as was usual. Susan and Sir Peter would dance it together of course, Lucy knew. Engaged, they could dance together as often as they chose. What was certain was that tonight there could be no escape for Lord Verrell and herself; at least once, dance together they must. As she expected, he requested the honour of the first dance. The movements being lively, it gave them little opportunity for conversation which was a relief to Lucy. And when opportunity did occur, neither appeared to have anything to say. Taking a cautious glance at Verrell's face at one point, Lucy thought he looked almost as grim as when they first met. It put the last smothering blanket on inspiration.

When the dance ended, Verrell, with a small *tch!* of what might have been annoyance, said, 'It appears, Miss Daunton, we have nothing whatever to say to one another when we are not quarrelling.'

Lucy lifted her troubled gaze to meet his. 'I'm sorry. I have tried to think of something – *anything* – to say but nothing comes.'

'The fault is mine. But I do have something to say to you. It cannot, however, be said here at this moment. It would be unwise, I think, to keep the rest of the party waiting for our return. Perhaps later there will be opportunity to be private.'

Something to say to her that needed privacy to be said. . . . Was that why he looked so grim? All Lucy's fears rushed back. She had lulled herself into thinking that the savage promise he had made her had been an expression of anger, without real intention behind it. Perhaps he *had* meant it. What else could account for his serious manner, his forbidding look? He intended to give her the warning he had promised her. But why tonight?

Here? Where there were so many reminders of their first meeting! The cruelty of it seemed to link with that of his threat. If she was silent before, she was utterly dumb now.

Looking down at her bent head, Verrell wished he could see her expression. How had she had received his words? Was she unwilling to hear what he might have to say, especially in the more private circumstances at which he had hinted? Further words at this moment might complicate matters beyond their present state and he decided to say no more for the time being.

He regretted that decision soon after making it. When they returned to where Mrs Gresham and Mrs Rothwell were sitting, it was to find Richard Tarrant with them and to witness the smiling pleasure and, he could have sworn, the relief, with which Lucy met him. Tarrant claimed the next dance with her and the two went off together as soon as it began to form. Verrell did what was expected of him and invited Susan to partner him. A second dance with Miss Daunton was all that convention allowed him and doggedly, he resolved to make sure of it as soon as possible.

He soon discovered that Tarrant had already laid claim to the one remaining waltz to be danced that evening in this conservative neighbourhood, but since *dancing* with Miss Daunton was not his chief object, Verrell was not concerned. A country dance better suited his purpose and Lucy accepted his invitation to dance the boulanger a little later. It was done with a grave look very much in contrast with the happy readiness with which she had accepted Tarrant's invitations.

When the time came for them to take their places, she laid her hand on his arm and walked steadily beside him but took care not to look at him. Verrell waited only until they reached the point furthest from their party before guiding her to the edge of the room. *Tread softly. . . speak gently*, Julia had said, but the words he spoke sounded stiff and cold in his own ears. 'Will you come with me now where we can be private?'

Lucy had steeled herself to meet with dignity whatever was to come. Her head held high, firmly and quietly she said, 'Yes.'

'Thank you.' He took her arm and guided her into the passage that led to the lesser rooms.

He did not choose the place deliberately: a door stood open and he steered her into the room beyond before he recognized it as one only too memorable to them both.

On this warm summer evening there was no fire to glow and glitter in the reflective surfaces. The curtains were undrawn but the sun was down and the room was slipping away into a dusk that softened its contours and lent it a touch of mystery.

Verrell closed the door on them and then stood for a moment looking at her without speaking. Though she was paler than usual, he thought she had never looked prettier. No longer in mourning, her gown was the required white for young girls, something light and gauzy, trimmed with flame-coloured ribbons that suited her colouring. She wore, too, a necklace of amethysts, a matching bracelet and a hair ornament. Had he seen her wearing them before? Something saved from the ship-wreck to which her father had brought her? He could not remember.

Abruptly, he asked, 'Does it trouble you to be in this particular room with me again? I did not bring you here by design.'

Facing, as she thought, one of the worst moments she had yet had to face, she had steeled herself to keep firm hold on her nerves and met his gaze with steady determination. With no more than a faint hint of bitterness, she said, 'Where we are does not matter. Please say what you have to say.'

He frowned, checked momentarily by her tone, then said slowly, 'First about that original occasion—'

'Yes?' she prompted as though this opening was not unexpected.

'It may be difficult for you to understand, but it was myself with whom I was angry when I came into this room. I had just come from insulting Peter Eddis, whose guest I was at the time. I can only suppose that seeing an opportunity to discharge my guilt on to someone else, I seized it.'

'Anthony Daunton's daughter. Yes, I understand. And now?'

Far from being receptive to what he was saying, he felt she was facing him like a duellist whose defending rapier was ready to oppose him at every point. He turned from her, took one quick step away, turned back. 'What is it? Are you remembering my attempt to terrify you in Juba's pen? *Did* I terrify you?'

She looked at him strangely. Answered honestly, 'If it pleases you to know it, yes, you did.'

'*Pleases me*! Good God! Afterwards, I was never so bitterly ashamed of anything I had ever said or done!' His frown deepened. 'If you can think *that* – what in heaven's name are you expecting from me now?'

She said stiffly, 'Are you not intending to – to fulfil the promise you made then? To give me the warning you promised?'

Where were his wits? Why had he not anticipated that this was what she would be expecting? '*No!*' he said emphatically. 'My purpose here is the very opposite! To try and undo the mischief done by my accursed words and temper. To have said what I did to a girl half my age – little more than a child—'

'I am past nineteen years of age and less of a child than I was, Lord Verrell. I have grown up quite a lot in the fifteen months that have passed since my father died.'

That he had contributed to that growing up, he could be sure. And in no pleasant way. The thought dammed up speech and they stood looking at each other in memory-haunted silence, the shadows deepening round them. On an impulse, though hesitantly, Lucy said at last, 'After you left – after I left the stables that time – I realized you had not been angry when you first came in. It occurred to me that perhaps it was-it was my awkwardness, my fears that made you so.' She was far from certain he would understand.

It seemed he did. 'Heaven knows, I had given you reason enough for them!' Self-disgust rang clear in his tone.

'But – but it did not seem to me altogether unreasonable that you should want to retaliate in some way for the – the injury my father had done you. And since he was not at hand and I was—' She shrugged. 'It seemed to be all one with the fact that you had come to live in Chalworth – bought my – bought Herriards. I—' Her voice faltered to a stop.

'When I bought Herriards I did not know you still lived in Chalworth. I was in a hurry to settle the matter of where I should live when I returned from winding up my affairs in India. I knew and liked Herriards. It was largely a matter of convenience.'

'Oh.'

'But you were right about my seeing that you thought you had reason to fear me when we first met. Stupidly, I let it anger me. I have been sadly off-balance ever since I set foot in England again. The life I lived in India and Burma was very different from that lived here.' He reached for one of her hands and held it in a warm clasp. 'I have given you a lot to forgive. Do you think it possible for us to put the past behind us and let this occasion serve as a first meeting?'

She gave him a long wondering look. 'Recently I found myself wishing we might do that. Wishing that we might meet without being burdened by – by things that cannot be changed.'

Surprised, he said slowly, 'You are generous beyond my deserving, Miss Daunton. If that is what you wish, that is how it shall be.' He raised her hand to his lips and kissed it lightly. 'A *thank you* and a seal on our pact.' He did not immediately release her hand but smiled down at her in the way she had seen only once before. 'And you will remember Juba, won't you?'

She nodded.

'Then, as earlier, I think we should return to our friends before the length of our absence makes them inquisitive.'

They found Richard Tarrant still with their group. Neither he, nor any of the others commented on the length of time they had been absent, but Richard's unrevealing gaze lingered on them a little longer than that of anyone else.

Refreshments were served in two rooms adjoining the ballroom and to one of these the party now went. When they returned to the ballroom it was to find that the waltz was to be the next dance. As Lucy walked with Tarrant on to the floor, he said with soft amusement, 'I am relieved to see you smiling, Miss Daunton. You went out to your last dance like a queen going to her execution. I will allow though, that you returned with the look of one who had made a passably satisfactory treaty. It was the second interesting encounter between you and Lord Verrell that I have witnessed and I confess to being quite vulgarly curious.'

Just for a moment Lucy was at a loss as to how she should answer him, but then, following his lead of light amusement she stared past him and said, 'There is a very pretty girl looking at you in a most interested way, Mr Tarrant.'

He did not look round but kept his smiling gaze on her, his green eyes narrowed and gleaming. 'If I believed you I don't doubt I would be flattered. As it is, I am content to be dancing with the prettiest girl in the room. I accept your charmingly delivered reproof, and concede that how you and Lord Verrell deal together is no business of mine. I shall do my best to master my shameful curiosity.'

'Do you always watch people so closely?'

'By no means. Only those who hold my attention.'

Lucy slanted a saucy look at him. 'Lord Verrell would be flattered.'

He laughed. 'That deserves punishment. In time I shall think of something appropriate.'

Her mood already lightened by the outcome of her meeting with Lord Verrell, Lucy's spirits rose higher. Who could fail to respond to Richard Tarrant's light banter, his easy manner, his steady good humour? The colour returned to her cheeks, her eyes sparkled and no one observing her and her partner could miss noticing that they were well pleased with one another.

CHAPTER SEVENTEEN

The weather changed. Smiling June gave way to scowling July. Chill winds blew, clouds prevailed, showers of rain were frequent. In the late afternoon of the last day of the first week, Lucy offered to deliver a promised note belatedly remembered by Mrs Rothwell. The latest shower had not long ended, gathering clouds were already threatening another and creating a false dusk.

Lucy hurried as quickly as she dared over the cobbles of the main street made slippery by the rain, thankful she had only a short distance to go. Susan, who might have been with her, had gone into Surrey with Sir Peter to stay with his sister in Haslemere and meet other members of his family. It was Sunday and the street was empty, no one who need not do so was venturing out into this uninviting gloom. Later, perhaps, the evening service might draw the stout-hearted to church.

Her note delivered, Lucy was about to recross the street when she heard the clip-clop of a horse's hooves on the stones coming at an easy pace. Shadowy in the poor light, she saw a horse and rider approaching from the south and waited for them to pass. From behind her, something that might have been a ball but by its irregular shape was more probably a blown-up bladder, shot out past her, snaking erratically along the ground immediately before the horse. Scampering after it came a small boy who, belatedly realizing his danger, came to a halt right under the horse's hooves so it appeared to Lucy. It seemed impossible that the child would not suffer injury or worse. With a shrill whinny, the horse reared, there was a stamp and slither of hooves and then horse and rider were down. The boy, astonishingly unhurt, took to his heels and vanished into the alley from which he had come.

The horse was making efforts to rise as Lucy reached it but the rider lay still. Afraid the horse might roll and add to whatever damage the rider had sustained, Lucy put all her strength into trying to drag him clear. Small as her success was, it was enough. The animal heaved itself up, stood for a moment blowing hard before shaking its head and clattering away.

It was Lord Verrell who lay unconscious at her feet and Lucy could see the deeper darkness of blood smearing the rain-dark cobbles between where his head had lain originally and where it lay now. Praying someone would come on the scene to help her, she knelt down beside him to remove his cravat to make a pad for the wound.

The only person who came was a girl whom Lucy vaguely recognized as one of a numerous family and who, most probably, was an older sister of the cause of the accident. She had been sent, Lucy guessed, to try and make sense of whatever frightened report her sibling had made. Seeing a man stretched unconscious on the ground, Lucy suspected she was quite as ready as her brother to take to her heels.

Snapping an imperative, '*Come here!*' she followed it with a gentler, 'I need your help.'

The girl hesitated, shuffling her feet, and Lucy, desperate for help, snapped again, 'Remember it was your brother who caused the accident and the more you can do to help the better.'

Brought up in the fear of powerful authority the child crept to her side.

She was about nine or ten years old, Lucy saw, poorly dressed, a limp pink ribbon tying back her hair, probably a concession to 'Sunday best'.

'I need you to go to Herriards as fast as you can and bring help. Go to the house and say Lord Verrell has had an accident and they need to send the means to carry him home. Can you remember that?'

She heard the girl's gasp of horror on hearing the unconscious man's identity and then her frightened, 'I dursn't, miss! Oh, I dursn't! Them people would never listen to me!'

Her hands busy, Lucy said as patiently as she could, 'Then go to the stables and find one of the grooms. If his lordship's horse has returned to his stable, they may be preparing to come and look for him. But find *someone* and give him the message. And *hurry!*'

Spurred into compliance by the commanding tone, the girl at last ran off in the right direction.

Lucy was sitting on the damp cobbles now, with Verrell's head in her lap, his freely bleeding wound padded by his cravat and her shawl. She listened achingly for the first sounds of approaching help as the long minutes passed. Every now and then she slipped her hand inside his jacket to feel for the slight rise and fall of his chest that told her he was alive.

An added worry was the blackness of the clouds bunching lower and lower overhead threatening to release another deluge before help arrived. She watched Verrell's face anxiously, fretting at her inability to do more than she had done. It was strange to be able to study his features at such close hand and without his knowledge. The lines of harsh experience showed less clearly in his unconscious face, so that a certain sensitivity in it became more noticeable. At this moment it was the face of a man she might have liked if they had met in a more usual way. Did he remember, as she did, their agreement to forget the past?

She wondered what he had been like as a young man? How had he felt when he found himself threatened with a charge of murder? And then realized he was in positive danger of being hanged for it and knew he must leave his home and family and go to a distant country and there find a means to keep himself alive? *Could* he forget what had happened to him? Could *she* forget it was through her father it had happened?

Because she was keeping anxious watch on him, she saw the first slight tremor of his eyelids, a hint that he was beginning the journey back to consciousness. Her impatience mounted. How long had the girl been gone? Surely someone must come *soon*! And then at last, she heard distant sounds coming from the right direction.

The first to reach her was her messenger. 'Couldn't find no one first off, miss,' she breathed hoarsely. 'But they're coming now.'

And out of the gloom there emerged four men carrying an improvised stretcher and horse blankets.

'What happened, miss?' That was Naylor, the head groom.

She gave him a brisk outline, ending, 'He'll need a doctor. He has a wound at the back of his head. It's still bleeding, I think.' She held the padded cravat and shawl in place as the men lifted Verrell carefully on to the makeshift stretcher. Even as the blankets were settled over him, the first drops of rain began to fall.

'We'll need to be quick, before we get the full downpour. Thank you for what you have done, miss,' Naylor said. 'We'll look after him now.'

She stood watching the small procession move away down the street towards Herriards until it was veiled from sight by the steadily increasing rain. Though she had been praying for help to come, perversely, she now found herself resenting the loss of her charge. It was surprisingly important to her to know how he went on and that he had not suffered any great or lasting damage.

It was the chill of the rain soaking through her unprotected gown that at last drove her to turn and hurry back to the rectory, there to explain her late return and her soaked and shawlless condition.

The rector called at Herriards early the next morning to enquire how his lordship did. He was shown into the smaller drawing-room where Verrell and Mrs Gresham were sitting together. His lordship, looking pale, confessed to a headache but nothing worse.

'Seven stitches in his scalp, Mr Rothwell, and in need of a few in his temper because I have persuaded him to sit quietly with me this morning,' Julia Gresham said with a smile.

'A fall from my horse is no great matter and not the first I have had,' Verrell, a testy patient, said.

'But at a guess, not on to Chalworth's cobbles,' his aunt returned.

Verrell shrugged that aside. 'What concerns me more is the vague memory I have of a child being involved. Whose I do not know. Nor whether it was hurt. Have you heard anything, Rector?'

'Miss Daunton mentioned a child, a young boy, chasing something like a ball. It was he who caused the accident. She said, too, the boy was unhurt thanks to the speed of your reaction. It was that which caused your horse to rear and slip on the wet cobbles bringing you both down. I will discover which of the village children it was, if you wish.'

'Only to the point of being sure the child was not hurt.'

'Miss Daunton was sure he was not.'

'Then there is no need for more.'

'Miss Daunton behaved very sensibly. Sending for help, staunching the blood with what was to hand,' Mrs Gresham put in swiftly.

'My cravat and her shawl, so Naylor told me.' Verrell spoke drily. 'He mentioned, too, that she was sitting on the damp cobbles nursing my ungrateful head in her lap.'

'The shawl! I had almost forgotten,' Mrs Gresham said. 'Will you give Miss Daunton our thanks and apologies. Mrs Penfold has done her best with it, but fears it will not be what it was. Blood is so very difficult to deal with.'

Within a short time of the rector taking his leave, a servant set out from Herriards for Tilchester carrying behind his saddle a sad-looking, still damp shawl. His instructions were to bring back a selection of shawls similar to, or better than, the sample.

Lord Verrell came to the rectory the next day with the chosen replacement. Little as Lucy wanted to be thanked for what she had done, she managed to receive his thanks creditably. Lord Verrell on the other hand, was stiffly formal. The accident, it seemed to her, had set their new-found cordiality back a step.

Two days later, she caught a glimpse through one of the rectory windows of his lordship riding by. He was heading south out of Chalworth and recollecting her promise to visit Juba, she decided that this was as good a time as any to keep her promise and visit the dog.

She was a little delayed by Mrs Rothwell needing her help winding into balls some newly arrived skeins of wool, but it was soon after two o'clock when she set out.

On the carriageway, between the gates and the house, she met Mrs Langley and her niece just leaving. Miss Wynn was looking very smart in a blue-striped muslin gown and a jaunty straw hat tied on with primrose ribbons. Having exchanged courtesies, with a telling glance at Lucy's plain round gown, Miss Wynn asked, 'Are you calling on Mrs Gresham?'

'No, I am visiting Juba.'

'Jubal?' Miss Wynn's eyebrows expressed her puzzlement.

'No, Juba. In the stables. A dog.'

'Oh.' Miss Wynn had nothing to say about such an odd intention and instead set about making clear her own superior position.

Knowing nothing of local history, she asked airily, 'Do you know the house? Such a charming old place. We have had a most delightful visit. Mrs Gresham showed us the kindest attention . . . seemed very pleased to renew her acquaintance with me. She showed us all the principal rooms and some of the curiosities.' She frowned at her aunt who had twice tugged at her sleeve in an effort to stem the flow. Refusing to be deflected, she plunged on, 'And then Lord Verrell came in and when I remarked on the delightful view from the drawing-room window nothing would do but for him to show me around the gardens even though he had said he was about to ride out on business. I could not help but feel I was a great favourite with them both.' She glanced through her lashes to see how this information was received.

'Why should you not be?' Lucy said co-operatively, which did not satisfy Miss Wynn who had hoped for some sign of envy or chagrin. Before she could summon up further evidence of her value to Lord Verrell and his aunt, Lucy, suddenly quite certain she did not like Miss Wynn, said, 'But I must not keep you,' and with a small bow, walked on.

CHAPTER EIGHTEEN

Escaping from Miss Wynn's importunities, Verrell had ridden the lanes around Chalworth with no purpose other than to pass sufficient time for the visit to end.

Naylor came to take his horse as soon as he entered the stableyard, saying with a jerk of his head, 'Miss Daunton's with the dog, m'lord.'

Verrell nodded and went to look in at the open top half of the stable door. The scene was almost an exact repeat of the too memorable first occasion. As then, the girl was sitting on a bale of hay with Juba's great head laid in her lap. As then, too, there was a look of idiotic bliss on the dog's face as the girl fondled his ears and talked softly to him. Though he was not aware of it, Verrell smiled with the same pleasure he had first known on that occasion. When he had last seen her he had felt something of a fool for landing unconscious at her feet when he and his horse had come down. Unreasonable, but there it was. Forgetting that now, together with his promise not to intrude on her visits to his dog, he opened the door and walked in.

Lost in thought, Lucy did not hear him enter, but Juba raised his head and acknowledged him with a perfunctory wag of his tail. She turned then, stared, said, 'Oh, I thought—' She broke off. She could hardly tell him she had thought him safely else-where.

His black brows lifted. 'Yes, Miss Daunton, what did you think?'

She remembered the promise he had forgotten. 'That you – – that no one – would come to Juba's pen while I was here.'

A moment's swift thought found him a possible way out of that hobble. 'But that was before the agreement we made at the Midsummer Ball. We are different people now.'

'Are we?'

'New acquaintance, with no past history,' he reminded her.

She thought he had forgotten it. Rising to her feet, she stood regarding him doubtfully. She had no wish to say or do anything to reactivate the discomforts of the past, but the rapid changes in his attitude to her made her uncertain of what he expected from her now.

Her look of almost childlike perplexity both amused and charmed Verrell. Yielding to the temptation of the moment, he bent forward and kissed her lightly on the lips.

That struck a spark and she said sharply, 'New acquaintance do *not* do that!'

'Oh, they might, if one of them was me. As new acquaintance we have much to discover about one another, haven't we?'

He was looking at her in a way she could not interpret; a way that set her heart racing. Annoyed with him, annoyed with herself, she said sharply, 'Then it must be a habit peculiar to you, sir. Gentlemen are not supposed to kiss ladies before – to whom they are not married.'

His smile deepened. 'It was a kiss given in friendship, I assure you. It is not my general habit, I admit, but I found it so pleasant I think it could easily become one.'

His manner was almost flirtatious, very much in the style of

171

Richard Tarrant, but for some reason she could not find the way to turn it lightly aside as she did with Mr Tarrant. It was too out of keeping with what she expected from Harrington Verrell. She felt an urgent need to retreat. But if she said she must go, would he immediately flame up into temper?

Before she could decide, recognizing that she was troubled, he stopped teasing her and said in a more ordinary tone, 'Are you ready to return to the rectory? If I assure you I am quite in my senses again, you will not refuse to allow me to accompany you, will you?'

Relieved, she stammered, 'No – I mean, yes, it is time I returned to the rectory, but no, of course I will not refuse y-your company, if you care to come with me.'

As though anxious to prove his claim to sense, he spoke only of Susan and Peter Eddis's engagement during the short walk through the village, expressing his pleasure and telling her that Peter had asked him to be groomsman at the wedding.

He declined to enter the house when they reached it, but charged her with courteous messages for the Rothwells and they parted at the rectory gate.

Alone in the bedroom, Lucy took off her hat and sat for a time on the bed, thinking over that meeting, unable to decide how she felt about it. He should not have kissed her, of course, but as light and fleeting as his kiss had been, there had been nothing objectionable in it. Clearly it had meant nothing to him and need mean nothing to her. But why should the way he had looked at her make her heart race as it had? She wished she understood him better. She had wanted their unhappy relationship to change, but the changes that had come about were confusing.

Part of the change was her own different feeling where he was concerned. It had begun when he and his horse had fallen and she sat on the cobbles with his head in her lap. Since then, the memory of his white, unconscious face as he lay helpless had risen in her mind all too often. Consciously and unconsciously, there had been subtle alteration to how she viewed him. Because of that change, the new Lord Verrell of her present acquaintance might confuse her, but she no longer feared him.

No doubt he had been right when he said they had much to discover about each other. . . .

The weather at last relenting, as soon as the garden at Southways House was considered dry enough, Richard and Martha Tarrant held an alfresco party. It was something between a breakfast and a luncheon party with tables set up in the orchard and music provided by a quintet imported from Tilchester.

There were no strangers among the guests gathered at Southways on the appointed day and if there were no surprises, there was the relaxing ease of everyone being acquainted.

It was a hot day, a brazen tinge to the western edge of the sky's splendid blue hinting at a possible thunderstorm later though no threatening cloud had yet appeared. The apple trees provided enough shade to accommodate everyone who chose to sit beneath them and with an abundance of tempting delicacies and cool drinks, the party was assured of success.

The meal at an end, some of the hardier guests dispersed into the extensive gardens. Lucy was standing at the edge of the orchard debating which direction to take when Lord Verrell approached her. He had spoken no more than a few words to her however, when Richard Tarrant came up to them and laying a light but compelling hand on her arm, said to Verrell, 'Forgive me, but I must rob you of Miss Daunton for a time. She is wanted elsewhere' He smiled blandly at the other man, drawing Lucy away even as he spoke.

173

Given barely enough time to excuse herself, as they moved away Lucy asked wonderingly, 'Who is it wants me?'

'I do.'

'You!' She was torn between laughter and indignation. 'But that was—' She did not know what to call it.

Smiling, Tarrant said smoothly, 'I could not help but notice Miss Wynn's anxiety to replace you in a tête-à-tête with Lord Verrell and because her wish worked happily with mine, as a thoughtful host, I did my best for her.'

Lucy shook her head at him. 'Such sophistry! And what about Lord Verrell's pleasure?'

His eyes brimmed with laughter. 'Miss Daunton! Such vanity!'

She saw the trap she had fallen into and blushed. 'You know I did not mean— Oh, you are quite impossible!'

'And you are quite adorable.'

'No, no! You know you must not say such things to me. Tell me where you are taking me.'

'To show you to my roses.'

'Oh, how prettily put! And how difficult you make it for me to continue cross with you, as I'm sure I should be.'

'Do you think so? I'm so glad you are not. Especially as I must confess to plagiarism. I have to yield credit to Sheridan for first putting the words into the arrangement that pleased you.'

'But you have the credit for offering them to me.'

'Have I?' He laughed. 'Then pray be as generous as you choose. I shall be happy to accept as much as you care to award me. But' – he stopped as they passed through an archway – 'here we are at the rose garden and, as you will observe, seeing you, they are mostly crimson with mortification or pale with envy.'

She shook her head again. 'Now you are being altogether too extravagant! I think you are laughing at me, Mr Tarrant. It is quite a habit of yours.'

174

'Is it? I think it must be because you are so young.'

'Why should that make you laugh?'

'Pleasure, my dear. Simple pleasure. Do you not laugh when you see a kitten or a puppy?'

'I smile, perhaps, but I don't laugh.'

'But you laugh at their antics. What they do. That is what I mean.'

'Now *that* cannot be complimentary.'

'It is entirely so. It gives me pleasure to watch what you do and how you do it. To hear what you say and how delightfully you say it.'

'I think you are in a very strange mood today and now that your roses have seen me, I really should rejoin the other guests.'

He stood looking down at her for a moment or two with an odd expression on his face before he said, 'You make me feel very old.'

She looked up quizzically at him. 'I cannot think why I should. There cannot be so many years between us.'

'If years were all that counted . . . But add experience and worldly knowledge and I am a veritable Methuselah to your spring lamb.'

'I suspect you are still laughing at me. But it does not alter the fact that I must return to Mr and Mrs Rothwell.'

He raised one of her hands to his lips, brushing her fingers lightly with a kiss. 'You are right, of course, my proper young lady. Are you always very proper?'

She did not think he expected an answer to that frivolous question and gave him none.

Tucking her arm under his, he took her back the way they had come.

Lord Verrell did not approach her again, but when there was

opportunity, Mrs Gresham came to sit beside her and chatted pleasantly about this and that. Presently she made some mention of the increasing heat of the day and the probability of a thunderstorm before it ended. Lucy was reminded of another time of storming rain. When there was a pause, she said, 'I do not feel I ever gave you all the thanks you deserved for taking me in when Hyram Smith brought me to Herriards last Christmas. Soaking wet and muddy as I was, it is a wonder to me that you did! You gave me such care afterwards, too, though I do not remember all that happened.'

Mrs Gresham smiled and shook her head. 'Oh, you are investing me with more virtue than I deserve! I was snug asleep in my bed when the gypsies came. It was Lord Verrell who carried you in and who, man-like, laid you, dripping as you were, on the green silk of one of the sofas in the smaller drawing-room. From which I fear it has never quite recovered. By the time I came down in my dressing-gown, as I had been bidden, I had very little to do. By then, my nephew had the whole house astir. The housemaid had lit the fire and been sent running back to the kitchen for a hot brick; Mrs Penfold had been instructed to strip and dry you, see you well wrapped in blankets and to administer hot chocolate and brandy; Naylor was putting-to the carriage and had orders to drive to Ashwick at speed and Christmas Day not withstanding, not to fail to bring back Dr Walsh. I was simply left to supervise anything more that needed to be done while he himself shaved and made ready to go to the rectory. It was my first experience of what my nephew can accomplish without once raising his voice or giving any impression of haste!'

Silent with astonishment, Lucy was aware of Mrs Gresham continuing to speak but had no recollection afterwards of what she said. When, presently, she was alone, she sat for some time guiltily reviewing past misjudgements. Fear had prevented her recognizing his good qualities: he had deserved better of her.

In the privacy of their bedroom that night, Mrs Rothwell said thoughtfully, 'Matthew, did you not think that Mr Tarrant showed Lucy a great deal of attention today? It reminded me that when he came to the last assembly ball we attended, I took the impression that though he did his duty by dancing with those he should, he came to the rooms chiefly for the pleasure of dancing with Lucy. Do you think—?'

Matthew looked at his wife with a twinkle in his eyes. 'I think it would be unwise to read too much into so little. Lucy is a very pretty child and naturally draws male attention.'

'I doubt Mr Tarrant has much interest in children, pretty or otherwise. He is altogether a man of the world.' Mrs Rothwell's tone was dry.

'If he has serious intention towards her, marriage would certainly be the best solution to her problems. Lord Verrell once offered me that as being his opinion, too.'

'Yes. So much is obvious.' She was silent for a moment, then, very tentatively, she added, 'Lately, I have thought Lord Verrell is not without interest in that direction.'

Matthew looked at her in astonishment. 'I think you must be wrong there, my dear. I have never seen any evidence of his having any particularity of feeling towards her. And the circumstances that link them are so much against it.'

'Oh, I am not sure that he is aware of it himself yet. But now and then I have seen him look at her in a way that seemed to me to suggest she is attractive to him.'

'As I said, men will always look at a girl as pretty as she is. It is one of the pleasures of life we foolish men indulge in.'

'She is nineteen years old. A young woman. I should like to think that before long there will come a man who will show a more particular interest in her than mere looking.'

Still amused, the rector shook his head at her. 'One wedding in prospect has set you hoping for more. We can only wait and see. But what about Lucy? Does she favour any gentleman in particular?'

Mrs Rothwell sighed. 'Once I thought perhaps Robin Bellmore—' But there has been no noticeable progress and I have come to think she regards him as no more than a long-time friend. It would be a suitable match, of course. Lucy is very reticent about such matters however, and I don't care to force her confidence. She certainly looks on Mr Tarrant as a friend and is quite at ease with him. But she has never shown a noticeable *particularity* towards him either.' She sighed again. 'I think she cannot feel especially drawn to any of the men she meets because she is wanting to advertise for a situation and has asked me if you would be willing to give her a reference. She feels that when Susan marries she will be in the way.'

'Foolish child! Far from it. She will help to fill the gap Susan will leave in our lives.'

'I said something of the sort to her, but I suppose we should remember, Matthew, that she is not a child. Perhaps she *wants* to go from here . . . feels a need to be independent.'

The rector frowned. 'Well, we have no right of control over her, but it is a dangerous world for a very pretty young woman, as she has already proved. We can only advise and try to delay what we cannot avert.'

CHAPTER NINETEEN

It was decided that Susan and Sir Peter's engagement was to be celebrated by a dinner-party, this being thought to offer the most comfortable means of making the two families acquainted. It also meant it could take place at the rectory which could not accommodate a dancing party. The success of the occasion proved the rightness of the decision.

With that over and the late September wedding less than eight weeks away, the rectory ladies' attention and efforts were given almost entirely to Susan's trousseau.

A Tilchester dressmaker was to make Susan's wedding-gown and Lucy, as bridesmaid, was also to have a gown made by her. It was something for her to look forward to as she sat with Mrs Rothwell and Susan, busily stitching hems and seams on the petticoats, shifts and nightgowns of the trousseau or threading ribbons and whipping on lace for their embellishment.

Musical studies were continuing for both girls, though the time was approaching when, for Susan, their continuation would depend on her husband. Susan foresaw no difficulty.

On the last Wednesday of the month, Lucy's session with Professor Lowson had been particularly satisfactory to them both and, as they walked into the hall in anticipation of the arrival of the Herriards' chaise, Professor Lowson said, 'You may tell Lord Verrell his protégée's skill continues to increase. A reward to both him and myself.'

Lucy was startled. 'Lord Verrell. . . ? Did he recommend me to you?'

'No, no. There was no need for recommendation. You had already been my pupil. I knew your ability.' The professor beamed at her. 'But as the one who pays your fees. . . .'

'Oh!' For a moment Lucy could only stare at him. Then realizing he was looking at her rather curiously, she dragged herself out of shock to say, 'Oh, yes. Of course,' and turned with relief to the door as the knocker sounded.

As the chaise drove sedately towards Chalworth, she listened abtractedly to Susan talking about the new song on which she had embarked that day. Never had the journey seemed to take so long as she sat in tense silence wishing feverishly she could tell the driver to hurry so that she might the sooner question Mr Rothwell as to who paid the fees for her music lessons.

But arrival at the rectory did not give her the immediate release from disquiet she hoped for. The rector was out and did not return to his home until late afternoon. With difficulty she held her impatience in check until after the evening meal, but as soon as he withdrew to his study she followed him there and asked for a few minutes of his time.

'You're looking very solemn, my dear,' he said, as he signed to her to take the chair on the far side of his desk.

'What I want to say . . . to *ask* you, is – is important to me.'

He smiled encouragingly at her. 'Very well. Ask away.'

Baldly, she said, 'Does Lord Verrell pay for my musical instruction?'

The rector's smile faded. For a long moment he sat in silence. Then, 'What makes you think he might do so?'

'Professor Lowson said as much.' She explained how that had come about.

'It is true. I am sorry that you should have learned it is so. Lord Verrell was particularly anxious that you should not.'

In turmoil, Lucy jumped to her feet. 'It is impossible! I must discontinue the lessons. There is no way I can repay him. You must see that. Indeed, sir, you must! And the chaise – I thought *that* was for your sake . . . for Susan's . . . . But when she is married—' Oh no! I cannot—'

'Lucy, sit down and let us discuss this quietly and in a reasonable way. I may say it went against the grain with me that you should think that *I* was your good angel. It was only because I recognized, as Lord Verrell did, that your reaction to knowing *he* was your benefactor would be very much what it is that I agreed to keep silent on the point. The unhappy fact is that I cannot afford both Susan's fees and yours at the same time. But I could not reject his lordship's offer to sponsor you, because I am fully aware that yours is the greater talent.'

'There is no reason why you should do any such thing for me! You have made it all too easy for me to accept the great deal that you have done when I have no real claim on you and I am truly grateful. But Lord Verrell is a different matter! Even in the ordinary way, how could I accept such generosity from him? And with all – all that lies between us, how *can* I?'

'My dear, you cannot take on responsibility for what happened between Lord Verrell and your father. I am certain Lord Verrell does not attach any such responsibility to you.'

Lucy sat down again, saying slowly, 'It is not just that. There are – other things. We – I have sometimes – quite often – misunderstood how he felt towards me. Have not responded to him in a way he may have expected. Or deserved.'

'I see.' He did not, but he was not surprised to learn there had

181

been undercurrents. He had been aware that, at times, there seemed to be a certain distance kept between them, but he was surprised to learn there had been active hostility. It did not seem to match with the fact that both had shown more than ordinary consideration when the other had need: Verrell when Lucy had been taken to Herriards by Hyram Smith at Christmas and again in the matter of the music fees; Lucy in rescuing Verrell's dog from the tinker and when Verrell had lain unconscious after he and his horse had been brought down.

Feeling his way now, he said, 'Then I think we must accept that Lord Verrell has behaved generously to you. Can you not now behave with equal generosity and allow him to continue in the belief that you do not know he pays your fees? It would, I think, be discourteous at this point, to reject his kindness and give up your studies. While it places a certain burden on you, greater awkwardness than you have already encountered might derive from any other course. It is, I think, largely a matter of whether you put your own feelings first, or those of Lord Verrell.'

Harried as she was by guilt for her misjudgements of the man, accepting anything more from him was made that much harder. But she knew the rector was right and in the end, with as much grace as she could find, she agreed to accept the situation.

Once again she was left in some dread of her next meeting with Lord Verrell. How was she to prevent her new awareness working upon her manner? Her look? If only she could be free of the many tangles that coiled about her since her father's death.

If only. . . .

By the end of August word was flying round Chalworth that the village was to celebrate Harvest Home in the old style this year. Not only was Lord Verrell reinstating some of the customs that made it a time of general rejoicing but, it was said, he intended adding one or two customs he had enjoyed as a boy in his home locality.

It was usual for farmers to help each other with labour or by lending wagons or wains at this busy season, but this year, not only were Herriards' wagons to be freely available to farmers in need of them, but the usual order of the Herriards' farms being the first harvested was to be reversed. Harvest, his lordship was reported to have said, was more vitally important to the smaller farms than the larger and therefore their crops were to be the first brought in, depending, of course, on their state of readiness.

It was arranged that when the last hay wagon rolled home there was once again to be a Harvest Queen riding on top and a harvest supper for all who had taken part was to follow in one of the Herriards' barns. The queen was chosen by lot from among the village maidens and by chance the honour fell to ten-year-old Polly Cantwell, the youngest of those whose names went into the hat from which the rector drew the lucky winner after morning service on the last Sunday in August. It was to discuss all these arrangements with Lord Verrell that the rector came to Herriards on the following day.

They sat in easy companionship, glasses of the original, dry, red-gold wine from Madeira within easy reach. The room Verrell now used as both a study and a retreat was small and sunny. It looked south over a stretch of lawn bordered by some fine old trees and its long windows stood wide open to the summer warmth and the scent of roses climbing the wall between them.

'It's good to see the old customs revived. They help to bond the community,' Matthew said. 'But this idea they tell me you have, of cutting the first swathe of your own corn . . . that's new to us and not one many landowners like yourself are likely to follow since mowing usually starts as soon as the dew is off the ears.

With such fine weather as we're enjoying that will be soon after sunrise.'

'It was a practice we followed at Mardens Hall. One that my father handed on to me when I reached my majority. I shall be present on this occasion, but Herriards' first swathe is to be cut by Nathaniel Bray. I have given over the honour to him as the longest serving employee of Herriards able and willing to do it.'

'Old Nathaniel! He must be eighty-four if he's a day!'

'Eighty-six, he tells me.'

'And claiming to be still able!' The rector laughed. 'It will surprise me if he can even lift a scythe these days. I recommend you to stand well clear of him. He's apt to be a bit excitable and I would not care to answer for what might happen.'

Verrell grinned back at him. 'Don't worry. We plan to give him a new sickle with his name inscribed on the handle instead, and he'll simply cut a symbolic handful in lonely state with none to detract from his importance and a cheer from us all when he's done. His great-grandson is to be close at hand to guide him out of harm's way before the reaping line moves forward. But he's to ride to the harvest-feast with the queen of the day on the last wain to come in so he'll get his full meed of glory.'

'And you, Harry, how expert are *you* at swinging a scythe?'

'Oh, I've used one in the past but I don't mean to try it again. I shall do no more than introduce Nathaniel to his great moment and then retire to a place of safety.' He slanted his dark smile at the rector. 'This year the thanks given in your church will have more heart in them. Last year's harvest was dismally poor. This year it promises well.'

'And the Corn Laws will ensure you a high price for your wheat.'

Verrell laughed. 'By now I should know better than to prick at you, Matthew. Yes, I shall get a high price for my wheat and few of the men who labour at sowing and reaping it will be able to afford the wheaten bread it makes. I am not unaware that the law that eases the post-war lot of farmers, bears unfairly on their workers.'

'A better Christian than I would not have made that point. At least, not to you. There are few other landowners or farmers who have not in these post-war days cut what their men are paid.'

Drily, again with his slanting dark smile, Verrell said, 'I have had the singular advantage of knowing what it is to go hungry. But to return to the matter of customs. . . . I see from the records Herriards did not did not pay you a tithe last year. Is it not usual here?'

'No. I waived tithes long ago. I have sufficient for my needs without taking anything from those less well off, or even from those better placed.'

Verrell looked at him quizzically. 'You almost persuade me to come and hear one of your sermons.'

'If you do, I hope it will be for a better reason.'

The smile they exchanged now was one of understanding and comradeship. It occurred to Verrell that they had slipped into the familiarity of first names without even noticing it.

The Harvest Feast took place in Herriards' large home-farm barn that normally housed wagons, wains and equipment. It ended with happy sighs of repletion, the most optimistic villager's expectation having been exceeded. What little remained of the barons of beef, legs of lamb, game pies, syllabubs, tipsy cakes and jellies had been cleared away to be dispensed the following day among the old and the poor of the village. Now the three long trestle tables and the cross-set table that had linked them at one end were being dismantled to make room for the dancing that was to follow.

Lucy had sat at the top table with the Rothwells, Peter Eddis, Mrs Gresham and, of course, Lord Verrell, the chief provider of the feast. She had given a subdued return to his greeting but not sufficiently so to do more than to provoke a momentary flicker of his eyebrows. She had been relieved to find she was not seated near enough to him at table to be in danger of needing to exchange conversation.

Later, standing in the noisy, merry bustle created by the dispersal of the tables talking to Abel Warner who was making her laugh with his description of the difficulties of hoisting Nathaniel Bray to the top of the hay wain, she was forced to step back rather hurriedly to avoid being hit by one of the table-tops being carried out of the barn by inexpert helpers. She collided with someone standing behind her and being off-balance, would have fallen had not two strong hands fastened around her to hold her up.

Turning, her face alight with laughter, the last notes of it still in her throat, she looked up at her preserver. Responding to that laughter, Verrell smiled, in the warm, wide way she remembered from some other occasion but could not immediately place. 'Like a ripe apple . . .' he said and added as she blinked questioningly, 'fallen into my hands.'

The speed with which it had happened gave no time for thought, or for her doubts and fears to surface and on the last burble of laughter, she replied, 'Indeed! I was fortunate to be caught.'

His smile held, though a glint – more mischievous than threatening – came into his eyes. 'There's a penalty. I must dance the first dance with the Harvest Queen and the second with Mrs Rothwell. But the third shall be with you. After that it is agreed that we – that is, the Herriards' and rectory party – withdraw to the house and leave our guests to entertain themselves without the restriction imposed by our presence. By that time, it is thought likely, the barley-wine and cider will be exerting its influence over many of them.'

The musicians were tuning their instruments and he was forced to leave her then to lead out the young Harvest Queen, scarlet with pride and bashfulness.

The meeting between herself and Verrell had come and gone easily and naturally, Lucy realized, and the spectre of who paid her music fees had not materialized. All at once, the carnival mood of the evening seemed to take full possession of her: past mistakes slid out of mind and she gave herself up to the pleasures of the evening.

CHAPTER TWENTY

Although only the third of September the bright day was chilly as Lucy walked the short distance between the rectory and Southways House to keep another engagement to take tea with Miss Tarrant.

Arriving at the house, before she could knock, the door was opened by a smiling Richard Tarrant. 'I saw you from a window, so here I am, door porter to your entry. Come in.'

He took her pelisse and bonnet from her and, having laid them aside, ushered her into the drawing-room and to a chair beside a comfortable log fire that scented the room pleasantly. Seating himself in the chair opposite, it appeared he meant to entertain her, though it surprised her that he neither explained nor excused his sister's tardiness.

The change in the weather disposed of, Lucy mentioned the recently demolished hovels in Slippy-Slosh Lane and Tarrant said, 'The local curs certainly enjoyed a field-day among the rats that were unhoused.'

'The human occupants must be very pleased to find themselves in their new homes on dry ground.'

'I would not depend on it. Or not in all cases,' Richard said drily. 'I should be surprised if there are not several who are as unhappy as were the rats and who would have preferred to have been left to enjoy their familiar miseries. There are always some who find it pleasant to have something about which they can grumble.'

'But those ancient cottages were quite ruinous, besides dripping with water. I cannot believe anyone would want to remain in one if they need not.'

He smiled at her in a way she was beginning to think he kept especially for her. 'The difference in our beliefs is that you are young enough still to have faith in the good sense of those around you, while I, with longer experience of human nature, do not.'

'Well, I think Lord Verrell an excellent landlord who deserves to be appreciated.'

He laughed. 'Oh, indeed! A veritable paragon.' Softening the gibe, he added, 'Don't think I don't mean it – I do. He is fortunate to be wealthy enough to afford his generosity. Even so, not every landlord who is would follow his example. Now tell me, do I have a small niche anywhere in your pantheon of saints?'

'I did not say Lord Verrell is a *saint*. Only that he is a good landlord.' She looked at him quizzingly. 'Are you a landlord?'

'No, my dear, I'm not. But I could be a paragon in other ways. A very insignificant one, of course. Or don't you think that possible?' He lay back in his chair, utterly relaxed, his smile quizzing her now.

Familiar with his teasing, she felt herself on firmer ground, she smiled back at him, unaware that the mischief in her look brought her dimples into play. 'I don't know how it is, but something tells me you are not.'

He regarded her with gleaming eyes for a long moment before he said, 'You're quite right: I'm not.'

Something crackled beneath the lazily spoken words however

and suddenly she was less certain. Had she been impertinent? She had not meant to be, but there was, after all, something close to ten years difference in their ages. *Something* in his mood puzzled her. It was as though their relationship had undergone a change that she did not yet recognize. She glanced uneasily at the little clock on the mantelshelf wishing Miss Tarrant would come in.

Tarrant correctly interpreted the glance and with no alteration in the quiet conversational tone in which he had spoken so far, said, 'My sister has gone to Tilchester.'

Lucy looked at him in astonishment. 'Tilchester! But – did she not get my note accepting her invitation?'

'Yes. But later I told her that there had been a verbal message sent to say you were unable to keep the engagement.'

Bewildered, she stared. 'But *why*?'

He rose to his feet with lithe ease and reaching for one of her hands pulled her to her feet to face him. 'Because, my dear little Lucy, I wanted no interruption to what I have to say to you. By now you surely must have guessed how enchanting I find you. How deep in love with you I am.'

'No.' She was shocked. 'Oh, no! I thought that – that you *liked* me, but—'

'My dear innocent! My feeling for you goes far beyond liking. I am *obsessed* by you.' He saw her astonishment. 'You don't believe me? You should.'

'Oh, please—'

Gently he laid two fingers against her lips. 'No. Hear me first. You look on me as a friend, don't you? And as a friend you trust me?'

She nodded wonderingly.

'Then trust me when I say that what I am about to propose is in your best interest even though what I am leading up to is not

190

an offer of marriage. Only because, Lucy, it is not in my power to make you one.'

She tried to move away from him but he gripped her hands, holding her fast.

'Listen. Just listen. It is my misfortune to have a wife. We have lived apart for a number of years having discovered our total incompatibility on the wrong side of the marriage cere- mony. Mine was the greater fault. I married a pretty fool who these days thinks herself an invalid. She lives in Bath and will not stir from there. What I am asking, Lucy, is that you come to me as my wife without the parson's blessing.' Utterly serious now, he stared down at her with a look that demanded her agreement.

Distressed, Lucy shook her head. 'I cannot. Oh, indeed, I cannot!'

'*Listen* to me, Lucy. I am not trying to make you my mistress. It is truly as a wife I want you. If I can persuade Charlotte to divorce me, I will, but I've flown that kite before with no success.'

The logs in the grate shifted, sending a fountain of sparks up into the chimney. He moved his hands to her wrists. Still quietly, but with a note that throbbed through the quietness, he said, 'Think of the unhappy situation your father has left you in – penniless and dependent. Consider what your chances are of marriage with an equal. You will see – *must* see – that what I am prepared to offer you is better than what you can hope for. You have my word that if you come to me anything that is within my power to give you shall have. I am even willing to settle enough on you to make you independent of me.'

'Please, *please* don't say any more!' She stared at him beseechingly. 'You must see that I cannot do what you ask.'

A flicker of swift-changing expressions crossed his face.

191

'Because you don't love me? My dear, at this point I am not even asking you to do so. That will come. You will see. You have some liking for me, I think, and for the time being that will be enough.'

Her nerves were stretched achingly and it took all the courage she could find to say, 'I'm sorry, truly I am. Please understand. I must go.'

'No, Lucy. No!' He spoke no louder than before, but now there was force – even a kind of violence – in the words. He moved his hold to her shoulders. 'If you have believed nothing else, believe what I say now. I am not a man who easily relinquishes what he wants. If one way will not secure the thing, I find another. I have wanted nothing in life as I want you.

She *felt* the truth of his words, felt the strength of the hands holding her and began to be afraid, but was unsure yet of what.

When she did not speak, he gave her a small shake as though to drive home his words. 'Do you understand what I'm saying, Lucy? If you will not come to me willingly, I must put choice out of your power.'

She was shaken now, feeling breathless and a little sick. This could not be happening, could not be real. But the unpleasant thudding of her heart told her it was.

His voice thickened and deepened as Tarrant said, 'Martha is in Tilchester, as I told you, and I have seen to it that there is not a servant in the house. Though with all my heart I wish you would come to me willingly, if you cannot, then it will have to be because you will need my protection. Do you understand now?'

She understood. Her eyes wide with shock, she stared up into his burning gaze. 'No!' She barely breathed the word, not as an answer to his final question but as a refusal and a plea in one.

An expression that was almost a grimace of pain shivered across his face but left it set in exorable purpose. 'Then no more words. What I do now, Lucy, is because I must. And because I love you. Remember it.'

He drew her into his embrace and when she turned her head to avoid his kiss, freed a hand to bring it effortlessly back to face his. His kiss was fierce as though desperate for the response he could not draw from her. It lengthened and he slipped a hand into the neck of her gown to close on one of her breasts. She felt its heat, heard the altered, ragged note of his breathing and felt the fine tremble of his body against her own.

She stood stiffly in his hold, her mind clinging to the hems of hope for an escape she could not possibly plan. Raising his head, he held her a little way off to look at her, his face flushed, his eyes feverishly bright.

'For your own sake, don't fight me, Lucy. I don't want to hurt you. But if I must, I shall.'

As though her will had been leached from her, she drooped in his hands.

'Come,' he said again, and turned to draw her towards a nearby *chaise-longue*.

She moved listlessly with him as though half-consenting and his grip relaxed to a gentler hold. In that moment she wrenched herself away from him and speeding to a small table bearing a collection of ornaments, she snatched up the heaviest, a bronze figure, and hurled it through the nearest long window overlooking the street. The glass shattered, the first explosion of sound followed immediately by a jangling cascade of falling glass. Hardly aware of the jagged shards retained by the frame, Lucy leaned through the gaping hole and cried wildly, 'Help! Please help!'

There was a cart laden with bulging sacks almost level with the house. The horse shied and was steadied. The driver swung towards the source of the cry in time to see Lucy hauled away from the smashed window and, jumping from his seat, was into the house and into the right room in moments.

Lucy was fighting Tarrant now with all her small strength and the carter, a sturdy knight errant in muddy moleskin trousers and patched jacket, rushed towards them bellowing, 'Let young missy go!'

Tarrant swung round to face him, but the carter, a solid, well-muscled man of forty, wasting no further words, grabbed Lucy round the waist with one hand and landed a heavy fist in Tarrant's middle with the other.

Released from Tarrant's grip, Lucy found herself thrust behind her rescuer who showed every sign of being ready to make a fight of it if Tarrant offered. But Tarrant, winded, found breath only to gasp out, 'Do you know who I am, you clod?'

'I knows you for an incomer,' he was told, with all the contempt of a man Sussex born and bred. 'Miss Daunton didn't break no window for nothing! So we'll be going, 'less you wants to try stopping us.'

Tarrant turned from him to Lucy. In a voice of bitter reproach that revealed how far he was shaken out of his usual control, he said, 'You're a fool, Lucy Daunton. I would have given you all and more than I promised.' And with that he turned his back on them both.

Having hurried them out of the house, once they were in the street, the carter said, 'The distance isn't worth putting Major to the trouble of about-turning the cart, being as he's facing the wrong way. If you don't feel faint-like, that is, miss?'

Lucy shook her head. Taking her first good look at her preserver, vague recognition became certainty. In a small, trembling voice, she said, 'You're Mr Warner, aren't you?'

'Yes, miss. Abel Warner, that's me. Herriards' home farm.'

'I am so grateful to you, Mr Warner. You were so quick, so sensible.'

For all his forty years, Abel Warner blushed. ' 'Twas God's mercy I were passing when you dashed whatever you did through that window. And 'twas His goodness that the house door was on the latch. Wasn't much I needed to do after that. 'Twas plain as daylight you was meant no good by that incomer.'

Not wanting the man to think his timely help had been given in a poor cause, Lucy said, 'I went to see Miss Tarrant, but her brother had told her that a message had been sent to say I was unable to come. He had induced his sister to go to Tilchester and emptied the house of servants, too.'

'Ah!' The father of two daughters, Warner was satisfied to know she had not walked willingly into the situation from which he had rescued her. With natural tact, he did not ask to be told more.

Lucy was placing her feet with care and determination as they walked towards the rectory, aware that her companion watched her with anxious eyes as they went. If she as much as faltered in a step, she suspected that Abel Warner was ready to sweep her up and carry her the rest of the way. Reaction was setting in now and it would take very little to make her stumble, she knew. She was more than thankful when they stood on the rectory doorstep and Jessie had opened the door. She turned to take the carter's hand then and give him her heartfelt thanks again. 'I won't forget your goodness,' she said and meant it.

As she entered the hall, Mrs Rothwell came down the stairs. One look at Lucy changed her expression to one of concern and she hurried to put her arms around the girl, and say, 'My dear girl! What *has* happened?' The words released Lucy's pent-up tears of shock and fright.

Later, when her unhappy story had been told, she asked despairingly, 'What is wrong with me, that men – that men—' She could not find words for the question she wanted to ask.

195

Mrs Rothwell sighed. 'It's not *you*, my dear. It's just that you are so very pretty that men are tempted and I'm sorry to say some are predispositioned to take what they want by whatever means they can.'

Which was what Richard Tarrant had claimed for himself.

CHAPTER TWENTY-ONE

It was not until the following morning that Verrell was told the tale of Tarrant's attempted assault on Miss Daunton by his usual intelligencer, Joseph Naylor.

'You're sure of this?' Verrell demanded.

'Had it from Abel Warner himself. The young lady managed to shatter a window with something and cried out for help just as Abel was passing Southways. What was going on when he burst into the house didn't need no explaining, he said.'

Abandoning his intention to ride out, Verrell strode off to the rectory. As soon as he was alone with the rector, he said abruptly, 'I've just been told of Tarrant's attack on Miss Daunton. Is it true?'

'Yes,' Matthew said with equal economy.

'Will you tell me more, or are you going to stand on form and tell me it's no business of mine?'

The tone was harsh and Matthew let a long silence distance him from it before he said quietly, 'I think I should phrase it more diplomatically if I did, but there's no need, is there?'

Verrell acknowledged the reproof with a crooked smile. 'You have only to add "my lord" to put me even more thoroughly in my place.'

The rector smiled and made a small gesture towards the chair

Verrell had previously ignored.

Seating himself, Verrell said more quietly, 'Naylor told me as much as Abel Warner could tell him. I should like to hear whatever more you are willing to add to it. If you want a reason, it is because I am aware that your calling effectively ties your hands. There is nothing to tie mine. I want your permission to undertake what you cannot.'

'As the dispenser of justice?'

'If you like.'

'A disinterested righter of wrongs? Nothing more, Harry?'

Verrell frowned and was silent as though reviewing a point he had not previously considered. Then he said, 'Nothing beyond the belief that in this particular case I am better qualified physically than any other man in Chalworth. And you could say I stand to the village as its squire, which gives me some responsibility for what happens in it.'

Matthew had been watching him closely. Verrell appeared to believe the answer he gave to be true. He said, 'As it happens, Tarrant has forestalled you. He left Chalworth very soon after Lucy left Southways House. I went there yesterday evening but found only his poor distraught sister. She had returned from a trip to Tilchester to find the house emptied of servants, Lucy's bonnet and pelisse in the hall, a shattered window in the drawing-room and a note from her brother instructing her to pack up their belongings, close the house and be ready to enter the carriage he would send for her in three days' time. She does not yet know his address. I had the disagreeable task of explaining Tarrant's sudden departure for fear of the poor soul having it thrust on her in an unkinder way.'

When Verrell would have spoken, he held up a restraining hand. 'First let me tell you what happened as Lucy told it,' and went on to do so.

Verrell said grimly at the end, 'If his circumstances are what he said, his making her the offer he did can be understood. But to attempt to force her acceptance by rape – to plan for it! – was the act of a scoundrel.'

'That is beyond dispute. And much as you would like to bring Tarrant to a reckoning, for Lucy's sake it is as well that you cannot. Your intervention would cause more gossip, adding to her embarrassment and her distress.'

There was little more to be said about the matter and before long Verrell left. Returning to his study after escorting his lordship to the door, Matthew sat down behind his desk and stared thoughtfully into distance for some minutes. Was Mary right? Did Verrell have an interest in Lucy? His attitude to Tarrant had been vengeful but his anger had been cold. More bent on exacting an eye for an eye, Matthew thought, than the anger of an outraged lover.

But he was learning to take nothing for granted where Verrell was concerned: the man had surprised him too often.

In the two weeks that were all that lay before Susan and Peter Eddis were married, Lucy found it difficult to shake off a certain lowness of spirits. Her confidence had been badly shaken. She had liked and trusted Richard Tarrant, responding to him as to a kindly, teasing uncle. Now she wondered if she should have been able to make a clearer judgement of him? Had the flattery of his attention blinded her to his true nature?

She had misjudged Lord Verrell too, and though in the beginning he had given her reason for her to think ill of him, she gone on doing so long after she might have revised her opinion.

The Rothwells noticed her withdrawal into herself and unsurprised, said nothing, but left her to recover at her own pace.

*

Susan's wedding day dawned bright and clear, the air cool but scented with woodsmoke and windfallen apples. Susan, though a'twitter with nerves, was buoyed up with a happiness that lifted her into beauty. Her wedding gown was of cream-coloured sarsnet trimmed with turquoise velvet with which she wore a matching bonnet. Lucy's gown was of pale turquoise *mousseline de soie* and both she and Susan carried posies of small white roses.

It was a quiet wedding and a happy one. The bride's father conducted the service and the occasion gave noticeable satisfaction to both families. It was Susan's day and Lucy was glad to be allowed to fade into the background. Now and then, her attention wandered to Lord Verrell. Having hardly left the rectory since escaping from Tarrant, she had seen nothing of him in that time. That he had heard the wretched tale, she was sure, and she wondered if he thought she had brought it on herself. She remembered dancing with him in the barn after the Harvest Feast; remembered how easy they had been together and that they had laughed as freely and naturally as those around them were doing. Had it been for no better reason than having her doubts and fears laid to rest by the homemade wine she had sampled?

She studied him through her lashes when she thought his attention was fully engaged elsewhere. Perhaps now he was confirmed in his first estimation of her. If that was so, she was sorry with all her heart. *With all her heart* . . . The thought echoed queerly in her mind. She began to understand the direction of the change in what she felt for Harrington Verrell. To find herself in love with the man her father had made his enemy was a bitter irony. And the price of understanding came all too high.

It would have embarrassed her to know that Verrell was aware that he drew her notice from time to time. He wondered what

200

was going on under the soft black curls and behind the grave dark gaze. Her subdued manner did not surprise him. He kept his distance, suspecting that for the present, the last thing she wanted was attention from him or any other man. What Matthew had told him suggested that Tarrant had been strongly attracted to the girl, might even have loved her as far as a selfish, predatory nature allowed. It was the coldly elaborate plans he had made to trap her that earned Verrell's contempt.

He remembered telling Matthew there would be no personal satisfaction in bringing Tarrant to a reckoning, but the more he thought about it, the less certain he was that it was true. He would have welcomed an opportunity to express his anger and contempt physically on the man. The best he could hope for was that Tarrant, knowing himself to have been defeated by the resourcefulness of a girl less than eighteen months out of the schoolroom, was galled through and through by the knowledge.

Early in October, Robin came to the rectory alone. He was driving a handsome new phaeton, drawn by a good-looking bay horse. Putting forward his most charming manner, he asked Mrs Rothwell to allow him to take Lucy for a drive in it.

In such an open vehicle, an unchaperoned drive was permissible and Mrs Rothwell, hoping that after all romance might blossom between the two, did no more than warn them not to go too far and to remember the days were shortening and darkness would fall early on a dull day such as this was.

Lucy went willingly, even happily. Robin was too old and familiar a friend to raise doubts of his behaviour. He might steal an occasional kiss but there had never been anything intimidating about them.

Once they were on the road, she discovered Robin was in a mood that swung between buoyancy and fretfulness. She was not unfamiliar with this particular display of temperament. It was usually the result of his having been thwarted in some project and was generally short-lived.

Attempting to coax him into a happier frame of mind, she asked lightly, 'Have you heard from your well-connected friend of the spreading acres? Does he invite you for Christmas this year?'

She had made an unfortunate choice of subject. 'I've heard from him, yes,' Robin told her discontentedly. 'He is to be away himself this year. I shall not see him until the New Year.'

She tried again. 'And this splendid outfit . . . is it an early a birthday present?'

'Yes. From Grandmama. And pleasing though it is, it is also an obligation that I could well do without.' He scowled at his horse's unoffending back. 'I can tell you, Lucy, I had the devil of a job to get away for two or three hours this afternoon without saying where I was going and how long I would be after Jane's refusal to come with me! It led to words with the old girl and landed me fairly in the suds.' He shot her a brief look. 'Now don't turn your eyes up to heaven after I've put myself in Grandmama's bad books to come.'

'No, of course not. But I would rather you did not quarrel with Lady Vauncey through me. It is— Oh!'

Her words ended in a small shriek as the phaeton swung perilously on its springs as they turned a sharp corner. They were now on a long winding lane going deep into the countryside. It ended abruptly just beyond the tiny hamlet of Toxley, which Lucy knew, but doubted that Robin did. He had made no attempt to slacken his horse's pace, so speaking as calmly as she could, she said, 'There's a crooked bridge beyond the next bend. I think you will need to slow down for it.'

'Well, if that ain't enough! What is it with females that they must be forever telling a chap what to do!'

They reached the bend almost before he had finished speaking and at once were on the stone bridge. It had an awkward kink in its humped span and meeting it the body of the phaeton swung fiercely left, the right-hand wheels lifted from the stone paving and for several sickening moments Lucy knew that she was hanging over the fast-flowing little river in danger of being tipped into it.

It was a wheel hub grinding harshly against the stones of the left-hand parapet that persuaded all four wheels to reunite with the ground in the last moment before they left the bridge.

Cursing, Robin wrestled to bring his frightened horse down to a walk, while Lucy, badly shaken, took a deep breath to calm her quivering nerves. She had closed her eyes in those last moments, but when Robin did not immediately stop to inspect the damage, they snapped open and she saw why.

Ahead of them, a horseman had drawn aside into a field gateway to allow them to pass in the narrow lane. He must have witnessed the near disaster and was watching them closely as they approached. Robin, red-faced, realized it, too, and Lucy guessed he was anxious to go past before pulling up to examine the damaged wheel. With some dismay, she recognized Lord Verrell.

Robin gazed determinedly into the distance as they went by, but Lucy, unable to ignore his lordship, gave him a nervous glance and a slight bow. Returning it, Verrell might have found some humour in the situation if he were not so angry. The pace at which the phaeton had been driven on to the bridge had been suicidal and he itched to give the driver the dressing-down he deserved for putting his passenger and his horse at risk. He was, he recognized, the young man he had first seen dancing with Miss Daunton and who visited at the rectory from time to time. What the devil did the girl see in him apart from his looks which, though well enough if very blue eyes and curls appealed, as they might to a girl. But in his opinion there was sad want of a man's firmness in the youngster's face. He turned to stare after them until another bend in the lane took them out of sight.

Robin had turned at the last moment and seen the rider's continuing interest. 'Inquisitive fellow! What need for him to hang about staring!' he said, sourly, bringing the phaeton to a halt at last. 'Who was he? You seemed to know him.'

'It was Lord Verrell. He lives at Herriards now.'

'Oh, that fellow!' Robin lost interest and jumped down to survey the damage. 'The hub will need replacing and the spokes are a bit scored, confound it, but none of it is of great account.'

'Perhaps it would be best to turn back though.'

'Lord, no! Where's the need? We'll go on as planned.'

Annoyance was rising in Lucy. Robin had given her no apology for the danger he had put her in and if there was a plan for their outing, she had been told nothing of it, nor had her wishes been consulted.

'I have not yet heard of any plan,' she said, with unusual sharpness.

'Well, not a plan exactly. Just thought we would make it an exploring sort of jaunt.' Climbing back into the vehicle, Robin saw she was really annoyed and smiled winningly. 'Just thought how splendid to be out alone with you. Think a great deal of you, Lucy. Prettiest little creature this side of anywhere.' He set the horse in motion again, still heading away from Chalworth.

Lucy was not appeased. 'Robin, pretty speeches are all very well, but we must turn soon. Clouds are gathering in the west and the light will soon begin to dim.'

'Now don't fall into the dismals. I'll get you back all right and tight. But it's deucedly dull between these high hedges so we'll take the next turning we come to and see where it goes. Then we'll head back to Chalworth.' So saying, he flicked his whip at the horse's rump to increase its speed.

The lane they turned into was narrower and rougher than the last. Bordered by trees, it gave only intermittent glimpses of the lovely but lonely countryside and appeared to be heading towards extensive woodlands. There the light would be even poorer and Robin was still driving too fast for the rough surface over which they were now passing.

Robin had maintained a brooding silence for a while and when he spoke again, Lucy, caught up in her several worries, at first did not take in what he was saying.

'I expect you've thought about getting married, Lucy. Most girls seem to think about little else. What do you say to you and me taking off for Scotland? That would show 'em all, wouldn't it? It would be a great lark, too. Shall we do it?'

She came to with a sense of shock. He was talking nonsense, of course. His grandmother must have been particularly provoking to have brought about this prolonged, extravagant mood. But now the denser woodland was closing about them and she gritted her teeth as they bumped over increasingly rougher ground. She said crossly, 'Robin, will you please slow down. How can I take you seriously when we're galloping along like this!'

'We ain't galloping, though it is just what I should like to do. And why shouldn't I be serious all the same? Don't you want to marry me?'

On a spurt of irrepressible irritation she said bluntly what, otherwise, she might have said more gracefully. 'If you will have it, then no, I don't want to marry you!'.

'*What!* You don't mean it!'

Robin took his eyes off horse and lane to look at her, jerking the reins as he did so. Another tree root, standing proud of the lane's earthy surface, pitched the phaeton violently on to the already damaged side. The weakened wheel collapsed. Lucy was catapulted out of her seat and, hitting the trunk of a massive oak that topped the shallow bank, fell into utter darkness.

Robin had been flung across the tilted carriage to end half in and half out of it. Pulling himself up, he rubbed a bruised shoulder and clambered out to quiet his frightened horse. That achieved, he turned to Lucy.

She lay awkwardly on the slope of the bank under the oak, her straw bonnet crushed into a strange shape over her black curls. Even in the shadow here he could see the dark trickle of blood down one side of her face. He stared at her in horror. She looked dead and he was afraid to touch her. In all his pampered young life he had faced few harsh facts and now, thoroughly frightened, he could not think what to do.

It was Lucy's own fault, he thought angrily. If she hadn't been so tiresome, hadn't startled him by blurting out that she wouldn't marry him, this wouldn't have happened. It was all a game anyway and she must have known it. His grandmother would cut him off without a penny if he gave a hint of seriously considering it. She had said so often enough. Now they were miles from anywhere, the phaeton was useless and heaven knew what horrors he would have to face if Lucy was dead.

With shaking hands, he dragged her an inch or two into an easier position, praying she would show some sign of life. None came and tears of fright and self-pity came into his eyes. With excuses and complaints scrambling through his mind, he released the trembling horse from the shafts and tied the reins to a convenient branch. Already it was too dim under the trees to ride safely over the rutted, root-ridged ground.

Better to go back than forward, he decided, and tried to remember if they had passed any side track that might possibly lead to habitation. A vague memory of a track of some sort opening off to the right near where the woods began offered the faint possibility of its leading to a farm or cottage.

Stumbling over the tree roots that earlier he had driven over so blithely, he tramped some distance before he found the half-remembered track. Unpromisingly, it took him deep into the woodland, offering little hope of his finding a farm. He was on the point of turning back when he saw a glimmer of light ahead and, pressing on, came to a small cottage. An unshuttered window allowed the passage of candlelight and showed a line stretched branch to branch and hung with the melancholy corpses of long dead fox, badger, owl and magpie. He had reached a gamekeeper's dwelling.

Thankfully, he hammered on the door.

CHAPTER TWENTY-TWO

The coming of dusk brought anxiety to the rectory, but when the black gloom of a cloudy, moonless night followed and the phaeton did not return, anxiety turned to alarm. It was too dark to ride, so carrying a lantern, the rector walked the two miles to Lady Vauncey's home at Ashwick in the hope of obtaining news. Equally without news, the household there was in turmoil.

Having learned from Jane of Robin's intended visit to Lucy, Lady Vauncey was as much in fear of an elopement as of an accident. Stuttering with rage, she pronounced Lucy Daunton a scheming little baggage, set on trapping her grandson into marriage and was astonished to be told that it was to be hoped Robin's intentions were entirely honourable.

Nothing more could be done in the black of night, but there was little sleep for the rector or his wife that night and with first light, fresh enquiries were begun in every direction.

Lord Verrell going out to the stables for his customary morning ride, took one look at Naylor's face and said, 'Well, out with it, Joseph. I can see you're at bursting point.'

'Well, it's creating quite a rumpus in the village, sir. Seems that little Miss Daunton's eloped with the young gentleman that visits the rectory from time to time. They went off in his phaeton yesterday and no one's seen them since.' He bent to hold the stir-rup for Verrell to mount, but ignoring it, Verrell said, 'Nonsense! No one elopes in a phaeton.'

Naylor straightened. 'They're saying it's that or worse. That taken with what happened at Southways, maybe the young lady isn't as innocent as was thought. That maybe she's desperate to be married, situated as she is. And some are harking back to her coming from Pixham House on Christmas Eve the way she did, saying as it's all in the same line.' He saw Verrell's expression change and added hurriedly, 'I'm just telling you what's going round the village, m'lord. No smoke without fire, is what they think.'

'Just what you might expect damn fools and gossipmongers to say and think. It suits their way of enjoying themselves.' Verrell stood in frowning thought for a minute, then said abruptly, 'Saddle Bowman for yourself and follow me to the rectory.' He swung up into the saddle without help and rode off down the drive.

At the rectory he was met by a wan-faced Mrs Rothwell, the rector having already ridden out on another search. Quickly he explained that he had seen the phaeton the previous afternoon on the lane leading to Toxley and witnessed the near accident on the narrow, hump-backed bridge.

'A phaeton is not the best vehicle for rough roads and the way it was being driven makes an accident all too likely, Mrs Rothwell. But on such narrow lanes I cannot think they could have come to great harm.'

He wished he could believe what he said.

'But the lane does not go beyond Toxley and surely someone would have sent to tell us if . . .' Mrs Rothwell's voice dwindled into worried silence.

'Well, do not despair. I intend to ride there now. My groom

goes with me and if there is news to be had I will either come myself or send Naylor.'

He was gone before she could say a word of thanks.

The scatter of farms and labourers' cottages that made up Toxley yielded nothing. Turning back towards Chalworth, Verrell divided with Naylor the time-consuming detours to isolated farmhouses and cottages at the end of barely discernible tracks but without gaining any information regarding the missing pair.

Two wearying hours later, they were nearing the stone bridge again as they returned the way they had come, when Verrell saw the narrow, overgrown track on his right. It was all that remained unexplored. He had taken no notice of it when they were heading for Toxley and even as he looked along it now, he wondered if Robin Bellmore would really be foolish enough to drive into it in a light vehicle with darkness not far off. Judging by what he had seen of the youngster's driving, he decided with more than a little grimness, that Bellmore very likely *would* and signed to Naylor that they were to turn into it.

By the time the track entered the woodland, he was beginning to think they were wasting time, but for want of any other area to search in the locality, he pushed on further and within a short distance came on the wrecked phaeton. That there were no bodies lying beside it and no horse was all there was on which to base relief. He sent Naylor on to see whether he could find any indication that there had been forward movement, but the groom returned within a few minutes to say the track ran out not far ahead into a clearing used for the making of pales and stakes. There was no indication of a horse having gone so far recently.

They turned back along the track and at some point caught the scent of woodsmoke, found the side track and because they were now looking for it, finally detected a thin grey spiral rising above the trees. A good-looking horse tethered outside the gamekeeper's cottage gave hope of progress and handing his reins to his groom, Verrell went to the door. A slightly flustered game-keeper's wife opened to his knock and when she simply curtsied and stood back for him to enter as though the world and his wife could be expected in this woodland isolation today, he said with quiet grace, 'I'm sorry to trouble you but I think you may be able to give me news of some young friends of mine.'

Beyond her shoulder he saw Lucy lying ghost-pale on a box-bed in an alcove off the cottage's only living-room. Robin Bellmore, in obvious good health, stood in the centre of the room. Repressing a strong desire to knock him to the floor, Verrell said, as he passed him to reach the bed, 'You, sir, have a great deal of explaining to do.'

Lucy's eyes were open but the dazed look in them made him suspect that she was not fully conscious. Her face was ashen except where a bruise spread its darkness from her left temple to her cheekbone.

'Are you badly hurt? Have you seen a doctor?' Verrell asked.

Lucy heard him without taking in the sense of his words and her eyes would not bring him into clear focus. 'My head hurts,' she whispered and attempted to sit up, but was gently pressed back against the pillow.

'Be still. Everything will be taken care of. There is nothing for you to do but to lie quietly where you are.'

Something close to a smile turned her lips. It was not for any relief his words gave her, for again she barely comprehended them; it was something familiar in his voice, a note of vexation, that strangely, being something with which she was well acquainted, could be held on to in a world grown hazy and uncertain.

Turning from the bed, with a look of black menace, Verrell said to Robin, 'Outside, I think. We want no disturbance in here.'

Sulkily obedient to the authoritative tone, Robin walked out ahead of him.

At a small distance from Naylor and the horses, Verrell stopped and gripping Robin's arm, pulled him round to face him.

'Why has no doctor been called to Miss Daunton yet?'

'I've only just arrived.'

'Arrived!' The tone was ominous. 'And without a doctor? From where then?'

Robin shifted uneasily. 'Well, from home. I couldn't have found a doctor to come here last night. And this morning, for all I knew she was recovered.'

'Are you saying you left Miss Daunton here alone and injured and went home to your bed?'

The look on Verrell's face was making Robin increasingly nervous and he stuttered over his reply. 'L-Lucy seemed to be coming round a bit. There was n-nothing I could do for her and I knew they would be in an awful stew at home wondering where I was. My mother's an invalid and my grandmother—'

'You irresponsible young whelp! A young girl is injured through your crassly reckless driving and you abandon her to the care of people about whom you know nothing and go home to your bed! No thought of the imperative need of a doctor! No word to the Rothwells who had even more reason than your family to be *in a stew* as you put it! And with no evidence of haste you come this morning to discover if Miss Daunton is alive or dead!'

His words had the sting of a whiplash and the effort restraint was costing him was plain to see. He had not finished. 'Two things only prevent me giving you the thrashing you deserve – the fact that you are so much my junior and the distress it would give Miss Daunton if I thrashed her future husband.'

Robin's mouth dropped open. 'I'm not going to marry Lucy! I *can't!*'

212

'You think not? What other course is open to you, do you suppose? Miss Daunton has been absent from her home all night and, as the world already believes, spent it in *your* company.'

'But that wasn't how it was! She was here and I was at home.'

'If you think the world will believe that in preference to the scandal that has already spread abroad, you're as big a fool as you are a scoundrel. But get it out of your head that you are going to abandon Miss Daunton with a damaged reputation. I'll see to it that you do as you should, though God knows the girl deserves better than to have a contemptible young cur like you for a husband.'

'You don't understand! There isn't a chance of it. My grandmother holds the purse-strings in our family and she's made it plain there wouldn't be a penny for me if I marry Lucy. How would we live?'

'Are you saying you've always known this?'

Robin flinched at the menace behind the words. '*No!*' His voice was high and unsteady. And then, downscale and shamefacedly, 'Well, yes, I suppose so. But Lucy's so pretty and I *liked* her.'

The blow that felled him came so swiftly he did not see it coming. Verrell stood looking down at him for a long moment, angry with himself for having yielded to temptation, yet not entirely without some feeling of satisfaction. Then, looking across at Naylor, he said, 'When he comes to, put him on his horse and send him on his way. That done, ride to Ashwick and bring Dr Walsh here. I don't care if he's attending a deathbed, see you bring him! Then you can ride to Herriards and come back with the carriage. But stop off at the rectory to tell them Miss Daunton is found. Say she's hurt but the doctor is attending her – as I trust by then he will be. Ask Mrs Rothwell to join us here, if she will, and to bring a blanket. And all as quick as you can, Joseph.'

Lucy was again making weak efforts to sit up when Verrell re-entered the cottage. As before, he pressed her gently back against the pillow saying, 'Lie still. The doctor's coming.'

Through an open door at the back of the house, he saw the gamekeeper's wife feeding her hens. Dragging a chair to the bedside, he sat down and took one of Lucy's hands in his. He looked at her searchingly, trying to assess how near to conscious-ness she was, torn between a fear of troubling her and the knowledge that before long care of her would pass out of his hands.

Very quietly he said, 'There are things I must say. Do you think you are well enough to understand?'

She gave an uncertain nod and tried to steady her wavering gaze on him.

'I will be as brief as I can. This accident has left you in some-thing of a predicament. Because of what young Bellmore failed to do following it, it appears to the world – meaning Chalworth – that you have been out all night with a man. *Telling* them differ-ently will not be enough. Your only escape from scandal is for you and Bellmore to marry. I imagine you are not averse to the idea?'

She frowned, shook her head, winced and closed her eyes.

He took her response to mean she was not averse, which was the answer he had expected, yet he sensed there had been a reservation in it. Guessing at the reason, he said, 'I understand Lady Vauncey has some objections to his marrying you, but you are not to worry about that, I can persuade the lady otherwise.'

With an obvious effort to gather her forces, Lucy said distress-fully, 'No.' And then more strongly, '*No!*'

'What do you mean?'

Lucy opened her eyes and tried more desperately still to fix the wavering image of the man sitting beside her. 'Cannot – *will not!* – marry Robin.'

214

This time, there was no mistaking the positive dislike of the idea in her tone.

He sat in silence for several minutes before he spoke again. Then looking down at the hand he held, he said, 'Lucy – Miss Daunton, I mean – your situation is such that you *need* to marry. And marriage would solve other problems for you besides this immediate one. If you don't wish to marry Bellmore, will you consider marrying me?'

Her hand jerked in his as though the idea alarmed her. Seeking to allay her fear, he hurried on, 'A marriage of convenience, of course, arranged quickly and quietly. We could decide at leisure how to go on afterwards. Your marriage would silence the gossips, even though it was not to Bellmore. In fact, regrettable though it is, it would silence them more effectively . . . a title works marvellously upon public opinion.' His lips thinned in a cynical parody of a smile.

Lucy's struggle to retain a grip on reality and take in what was being said to her had taken toll, and strength to hold on was fast slipping away. The dark unstable world where she wandered through strange and often bizarre dreams was closing in on her once more. It was difficult to separate the real from the unreal. Had Lord Verrell followed his suggestion that she marry Robin with a second suggestion that she marry *him*? Was it likely? He certainly did not love her even if he did not dislike her as much as he had. He could marry where he chose: why should he enter a marriage of convenience? As for herself, with a clarity that shocked, she knew that such a marriage would destroy her now that she knew to what point her foolish feelings had carried her.

'Oh, *no!*' She gasped out the words with the strength of horror and losing her last frail hold on consciousness, fell into the waiting void.

Still holding her hand, Verrell sat quietly savouring the bitter aloes of that forceful repudiation. So much for Harrington, Lord Verrell! Not only emphatically rejected, but rejected with a repugnance that placed her opinion of him well below that of Robin Bellmore whom he himself held in contempt.

But why should he be surprised? Though he had never consciously intended her harm, would have thought it beneath him to have made any move against her, yet intentionally and unintentionally, he had made her afraid of him.

Sitting here lamenting her rejection was utterly pointless, he told himself astringently. He should be thankful for it, for what had his proposal been other than a misguided impulse of chivalry?

He was not thankful: he was mortified. Nor could he soothe his injured feelings with the pretence of having made a show of chivalry. He had been moving towards proposing marriage to Lucy Daunton longer than he had allowed himself to be aware. For how long now had he been watching with jealous eyes her happy responses to the pleasanter overtures of more sensible men? He loved and was in love with the girl.

Looking down at her pale, bruised face, what he felt now was infinite regret for what he had lost through his own stupidity. After a moment, he lifted the hand he held, kissed it gently and laid it beside her on the bed.

CHAPTER TWENTY-THREE

When a week had passed, Dr Walsh was able to say that if Miss Daunton continued to go on in a quiet, sensible way for a week or two more, all danger from the concussion she had suffered might be considered at an end.

Lucy's spirits however were slow to recover. Nothing had been seen or heard from the Bellmores. Robin had neither called nor written to enquire about her recovery. Even that small remainder from her old life had gone. Adding to her depression was her growing awareness of the sideway glances, the smirks and whispers that came her way. A shadow had been cast on her reputation and she was made to feel it.

Memories of what had happened after the accident came and went, some more teasing than others. She remembered rejecting Lord Verrell's suggestion that she marry Robin. She was less sure that he had then offered her marriage with himself – a marriage of convenience. It was more likely to have been one of her muddled dreams. But if that was what it had been, even in the lost and semi-tranced state she was in at the time, some waking nerve had known that such a marriage to Harry Verrell would be unbearable. Whether dream or reality, she knew she had exclaimed against it in horror and the improbability of it being real seemed confirmed in her recollection that when she next surfaced to a period of lucidity, it was not Lord Verrell who sat beside her, but Dr Walsh.

Mrs Gresham called to make friendly enquiries into her progress and brought fruit and flowers from Herriards' reviving progression houses. She also brought good wishes from Lord Verrell, which he might or might not have sent. He himself did not come. Later, when he and Lucy met, his manner was pleasantly courteous but there was a remoteness in it that suggested to her that the busy tongues of Chalworth's gossips were having an effect. She wished there could be a renewal of the laughing friendliness they had found at the Harvest Feast when they had danced together, but the promise of that occasion when they had seemed to find themselves so much in tune was never to be fulfilled or repeated it seemed.

She faced up to that as to everything else with as much courage as she could scrape together, endured the snubs of those who made open display of a change of opinion regarding her and was thankful for the Rothwells' loyal partisanship. The rector and his wife were too well-liked and respected for their protégée to be omitted from invitations, but Lucy found her inclusion often harder to bear than exclusion would have been.

Sir Peter and Susan, now Lady Eddis, returned from their honeymoon towards the end of October and the first visit they made was to the rectory. They came in the smart little chaise Sir Peter had commissioned for his wife's convenience. Susan's joy in her marriage was plain to be seen. She was looking very handsome, too, in a dashing green velvet Parisian bonnet and a fetching sable pelerine, gifts from her husband. Lucy was happy for Susan but was unable to escape feeling the contrast with her own less joyous state.

Early in November, the weather turned crisp and cold with light frosts silvering the rectory lawns each morning. One night, near the middle of the month, Lucy, who now slept less well than had been her custom, was particularly restless and eventually rose, wrapped herself in a blanket, and sat in the window-seat watching the stars or what she could see of the occasional wildlife visitor to the garden. The first narrow streak of light was dividing sky from land in the east when she saw a blacker, more solid shadow detach itself from the rest and after a brief tour of the garden within her view, take a position in the middle of the lawn.

Since his unpleasant adventure with the tinker, Juba had found few opportunities to roam. Perhaps, too, he had lost some of his zest for it, but here he was at this early hour, looking as though he meant to stay. There was no longer Susan's aversion to dogs to worry about but if no one came to claim him, it would quite naturally be expected by the Rothwells that as he had always been considered *her* visitor, she would be the one to return him to Herriards. Her reluctance to visit Herriards and find herself alone with Lord Verrell was greater than ever though her reasons were very different. If she went at any daylight hour there was always the possibility they would meet. There was little likelihood of his lordship visiting his stables before dawn however. If she dressed quickly she could walk the dog back to his pen before there was chance of it.

No one in the house was stirring when she crept downstairs. She took the old cloak kept for general use that hung beside a door leading into the garden and wrapped its woollen warmth around herself. She was thankful for its protection when Juba bounded up to her to give her as rapturous a greeting as ever he had. As good-natured as ever, he made no objection to her slipping a strong leather belt under his collar.

Though candlelight gleamed through chinks in the shutters of windows here and there, there was no one about in the village street. She had thought it possible she might meet a groom from Herriards looking for the runagate dog, but it did not happen.

Possibly having breakfast in mind now, Juba was as much her guide as her prisoner in the gloom under the trees bordering Herriards' driveway, but as they approached the stableyard, Lucy saw a glimmer of lantern-light showing through the tack-room window. Sure now of finding a groom to whom Juba could be handed, she walked in, only to come to a dismayed halt as Lord Verrell turned from reaching for something on a high shelf.

For a moment he seemed to be as confounded as she was, but recovering more quickly, he came towards her saying quietly, 'Miss Daunton, good morning.' His gaze dropped to Juba, his brows rising in wry resignation as Lucy freed him from the belt. 'Once again you bring home my straying property. Has he made a nuisance of himself to bring you out at this extraordinary hour?'

'Oh, no. He was just sitting on the lawn waiting. The way he does when he comes.'

'But how very early you must have been about to have discovered him.'

'Yes.' She made no attempt to explain.

'Dare I thank you?' He had seen her eyes widen and the momentary flash of dismay that crossed her face when she first saw him. It was not difficult to guess that she had placed some reliance on not seeing him at this hour of the morning. Not waiting for her to answer, he went on smoothly, 'His escape was probably my fault. A moment's carelessness with doors. My excuse is that we have had a worrying night with one of the mares in difficulty over foaling.' He gave her a slanting smile. 'He has such a decided fondness for your company, always making straight for the rectory if he escapes, I suspect he would be happier if he were yours.'

That prodded her into a too-hasty protest. 'Oh, no!' She heard the over-emphasis in her voice and blushed. 'I mean, I cannot think he would, even if you meant it, which I know you do not. Nor could I expect the Rothwells to keep him.'

'That closes every door quite firmly, doesn't it?' Careless from tiredness, he spoke sharply and immediately was sorry for it when he saw the momentary wincing in her expression. How young she was and how vulnerable she looked with shadows close to the colour of bruises beneath her eyes. Perhaps it was the shabby, oversized cloak she was wearing that made her look so noticeably young, for nothing remained of the schoolgirlishness that had once clung about her. He and Tarrant between them had added enough to her trials to put an end to that. And the trials she had faced would have defeated many a mature, experienced woman – or, indeed, many a man – but young and untried as she was, she had met them with courage. He wished there was something he could do to smooth her path.

'I'm tired and scratchy,' he said. 'Forgive my lack of grace.'

Lost in her own thoughts, Lucy was looking at him with aching intensity, thinking in a muddled way of the rugged, often unhappy path their relationship had followed and at the same time, *I must get away from Chalworth, avoid meetings like this, but oh, how hard it will be not to see him again. And how foolish I am to think so. . . .*

She said, as she seemed to have said to him so often before, 'I must go . . . return to the rectory.'

Though he had deliberately kept his distance from her after that humiliatingly fierce rejection of his proposal, now she was here he wanted her to stay. Trying to think of a way to delay her, he was inspired by the memory of his mare so recently in trouble and said, 'Have you time to take a look at the new little filly? Perhaps you can suggest a name for her.'

The double invitation made it difficult to decline, so she said, 'Yes, I have time for that. I should like to see her.'

They walked out of the tack-room into the first grey light of the new day filtering down into the yard and crossed to the largest of the looseboxes, Juba padding patiently behind them. Verrell opened the top half of the foaling box and Lucy looked in.

A lantern hanging from a beam shed a soft light on the bay mare who was dozing over her hay rack. Beside her, the little filly, a paler replica of herself was asleep in the deep straw.

'Oh, she's beautiful! And so is her mother,' Lucy said warmly. 'What is *her* name?'

'The dam? Freya.' He gave an odd little laugh. 'The Scandinavian goddess of love.'

'Oh.' She was disconcerted; wished she had not asked. Which was foolish, she told herself. She said, 'I-I shall need a little time to think of a name for her daughter. That is, if I can.'

'Do you not think Lucy would do very nicely?' he suggested.

She was thrown into deeper shyness. Flustered, she said, 'No, no, I don't think so.' Hastily, she turned away from the loosebox and he closed the door on the mare and her offspring.

It was full dawn now, grey and bleak and grudging of any promise of later improvement. As so often before, Lucy felt the need to escape from Herriards as quickly as she could. Without quite meeting Verrell's eyes, or intending to sound as formal as she did, she bade him good day, adding, 'Thank you for showing me the filly.' With more lightness, she told Juba, 'And good day to you too, sir.'

It was too sombre a parting for Verrell, but more impelled by a confusion of hopes, needs and wishes, he laid a detaining hand on her arm. 'Have you thought that if you chose to reconsider the offer I made you once and married me, you need not hurry away? You and Juba could live in the house I know you love and perhaps room could be made for me here in the stables. Then, when either of you were passing you could toss me the occasional tidbit of your attention. Just enough to keep me content. Nothing more.'

It was clumsy and and as soon as the words were said he suspected he had only succeeded in embarrassing her even more than he already had.

Lucy, made woolly-minded by tiredness and finding her emotions moving further and further out of control, said, 'Oh, please do not—' She was aware of the break in her voice and that her lips were trembling. She tried to cover her weakness. 'I'm sorry. I am not yet awake enough to – to respond to jokes.' She took a few agitated steps away from him as she spoke.

Holding up a hand apologetically, in a voice of such kindness her slender remnants of control were nearly destroyed, he said, 'Forgive my stupidity, I am half-asleep myself. It was not truly a joke, though. Believe me, if there were a respectable way to give you house and dog other than by marriage you might have them both, together with a kingdom, if I had one. As for my heart, if you had the least use for it, I would throw it in with the rest.'

She stared at him so long without speaking, he wondered if she had understood what he had said.

Her delay was to be sure that she did. He had said he *had* proposed to her before and in an odd sort of way he seemed to be doing so again. Or *half* doing so. She choked back a small slightly hysterical laugh: could one be *half* proposed to? But what he had last said was too important to her to be lost and quietly and carefully, she asked, 'Would you really offer me your heart if I told you I wanted it?'

'Dear girl, it's yours. You have only to take it into keeping.'

She could not quite believe yet. 'But before, you said "a marriage of convenience. . . ." '

'I thought it would make the idea of marrying me more acceptable to you.' He shook his head at his own folly. 'Though how I could be so witless as to think I could endure such a marriage is beyond me.'

Awkwardly, because still afraid of making a mistake, she said, 'Your heart – it was – *is* – all I want. Nothing else matters. Not Herriards, not Juba, or' – she found a tremulous smile – 'even the kingdom you don't have.'

Suddenly widely, watchfully awake, he stood very still, his gaze intent on her. 'Lucy, are you saying you will marry me?'

She nodded. Smiled tentatively, then shiningly, 'Yes. Oh, yes, indeed!'

He opened his arms and, joyfully, Anthony Daunton's daughter walked into them.